Lenny Bruce Is Dead

Lenny Bruce Is Dead

(A Novel)

Jonathan Goldstein

COUNTERPOINT
A Member of the Perseus Books Group
New York

Copyright © 2001 by Jonathan Goldstein

First published in Canada in 2001 by Coach House Books
Published in 2006 by Counterpoint
A Member of the Perseus Books Group

Counterpoint books are available at special discounts for bulk purchases in the
United States by corporations, institutions, and other organizations. For more in-
formation, please contact the Special Markets Department at the Perseus Books
Group, 11 Cambridge Center, Cambridge MA 02142, or call (617) 252-5298 or
(800) 255-1514, or e-mail special.markets@perseusbooks.com.

A CIP catalog record for this book is available from the Library of Congress.
ISBN-13: 978-1-58243-347-9; ISBN 1-58243-347-X
Canadian ISBN: 1-55245-069-4
06 07 08 / 10 9 8 7 6 5 4 3 2 1

For Buzz and Dina

AT MCDONALD'S, when I'm throwing out the stuff on my tray, there's a point where I get scared that my wallet could have been on there, too. I always think, as everything is tumbling into the garbage, that I might have tossed my wallet on the tray and forgotten. It always feels possible.

"I'll never do stuff like that when I'm a father," Josh said.

"You are a better man than I, Gunga Din," Chick said.

Josh thought that bachelorhood would mean he could wear dresses all day, but he never got around to buying any. He woke up at noon and watched *The Flintstones*. He played Air Supply's *Greatest Hits* while lying on the floor pretending to have a mental breakdown. He memorized Richard Pryor routines. He went out to buy beer in his sweatpants. He lay under the bed and pretended he was on Devil's Island.

At the bottom of the yogurt, there was something black and beetlelike. He suddenly felt a gob of vomit move up through his throat. It made him feel ten years old.

At the shopping mall there was a teenage boy who handed out pieces of paper.

"You are going to die," the papers read.

Those people thought they were getting coupons.

Josh's father, Chick, wanted to write a book about growing up in New Jersey and he wanted to call it *The Corner*.

Josh wanted to get his father started. He pulled a piece of loose-leaf paper from his binder and drew the cover. It was a picture of people yelling and fighting and old men sweeping. In the center was Chick and he was screaming with his hands over his face.

He pulled out a second piece of paper and wrote an introduction.

"The corner was where men met to play cards and fist fight," he wrote. "This is one man's story."

Before Josh sat down, he always checked the toilet water. There were stories of snakes that had crawled up miles of pipe looking for sunlight. Sometimes, right in the middle of everything, he would get up and look down between his legs.

Chick once told Josh about an old army buddy of his who went around kissing women on the hand every time he was introduced. One day he kissed the cherry on the end of a woman's lit cigarette. His lip was burned so bad he had to go to a speech therapist. It was one of his father's this-is-what-you-get stories.

Frieda, Josh's mother, would bring over food she made for him. Sometimes Josh ate it from a pot because all the dishes were dirty. He called it "cowboy style." When the coffee table was too cluttered and he had to eat it off his chest, he called it "deathbed style." One time someone came over and left a skateboard behind. He ate off that for a while, wheeling it behind him on a shoelace as he went from room to room. He called it "little boy lost."

Chick smacked his thighs, searching. Frieda called it the car-key dance.

"I REALLY, really hate you," he said.

"Now we're *definitely* not going," Chick said.

"It's incredible," said Josh. "With a photo novel you can get the same pictures as in the movie, but you take it at your own pace, and it's better than the movie because you can actually see what they're thinking. Like Danny Zuko might be saying, 'Yeah, I'd love to meet your parents, Sandy,' but the thought balloon tells another story."

"I have mice," Josh told his landlord.

"That's because you leave the windows open," the landlord said.

"That would only make sense if I had bats."

Josh's landlord was not a man of reason.

Frieda was going away and he wanted to fill her with hamburgers, milkshakes, and fries like it all was light.

Chick dreamt that they had made him the pope.

"I can't speak Latin," he kept telling them.

He sat in the park, all dressed up like the pope. He felt very lonely and depressed about it.

At Hanukkah his mother sent him latkes. There were no more paper towels. Josh ate them out of the empty cardboard tube. He pretended it was a Pez dispenser.

"My dad once took me to a movie when I was ten," Josh said. "It was Passover and we weren't allowed to eat popcorn. That popcorn smelled like God to me. God was right there and he was begging us to eat him."

He WANTED to be the man who entered strangely into people's lives, parking a car with foreign plates in their driveways.

In their kitchens, he would sit and wait for them to pour him a whiskey.

One day he would say, "I don't want to write about anything. I want to create consciousness itself; I want raw emotion." He would be wearing sunglasses and he'd be wondering if he'd just said the right thing.

Frieda told Josh a story about a boy whose father was going to take him to the circus. The boy was so excited he couldn't sleep the night before. In the morning he was very tired and excited.

It was only when they were at the circus that the boy realized he had forgotten to put on pants.

"What did he do then?" Josh asked.

Reggie's head was under the stall door.

"I'm looking," Reggie said, "but I ain't laughing."

"I ain't laughing," he kept saying. His face was deadly serious.

The phone rang. It was his father, who never phoned.

"Your mother," Chick said. "It's come back."

Josh sat down on the couch in his kitchen.

He and his father said nothing.

Out the kitchen window, across the courtyard, there was a girl taking off her shirt in front of the open bathroom window. It was the beginning of the fall. She watched herself in the mirror.

I can't believe it, he thought.

It was like that time the Ferris wheel broke and he was

stuck up there for three days. It was just like that. How they had to blast sandwiches up to him out of a cannon. How he kept missing and missing sandwiches until he got one right in his hand and he squished it and almost started crying.

HE BROUGHT out his frog like Kaliotzakis told him. Kaliotzakis was his best friend. He was also a maniac. When he talked about girls, he would smoosh his penis into the wall. Kaliotzakis once found a pair of old underwear on a driveway. He put them on over his pants and hopped around singing the Underoos song until his little brother Richie almost pissed his pants.

"The frog's gotta die," Kaliotzakis said.

Josh kept the frog in a yogurt container with a rock and some water in it. Kaliotzakis poked a stick in there. He made the same noise he made when his cock was against the wall. Richie was there, too. He was a few years younger than Kaliotzakis. Richie put his hand over Josh's eyes.

"You shouldn't see this," Richie said. He was crying. His father used to beat the shit out of him.

He thought Josh was pure.

Some of the girls thought Reggie looked like the Fonz. When things like that happened, Josh thought about how Reggie had been such a big baby in kindergarten, crying his head off and yelling, "I'm color-blind! I'm color-blind!"

So, there he was in the school yard staring at a caterpillar when Reggie came up to him.

"If you step on it," Reggie said, "I'll be your best friend."

Josh stepped on it before Reggie could even finish the sentence. He looked down at the splotch of light green juice and orange fur. He pretended he was thinking about something deep.

The Mini Pops were a group of children who redid popular songs of the day in their high-pitched little voices. People thought it was cute. Josh had one of their album jackets on the wall, and when people came over he would tell them that he used to be a Mini Pop.

"It was horrible," he said. "They needed to get me really sad for when I sang 'You Don't Bring Me Flowers,' so they would grab me by the shoulders and yell in my face, 'You're going to die one day.' The quiver in my voice on that song, it's from that."

But everyone knew he was just joking.

When Frieda's hair began falling out, the neighbor's little girl brought her over a baseball cap. It said "#1 Mom." She took to wearing colorful scarves around her head. She looked like an eccentric old blues singer. No one ever figured her for that type.

Chick taught biology. When Josh was eleven, he brought him to school on a professional day. He was supposed to help put the report cards into alphabetical order. Josh looked into the other classrooms and saw teachers doing their report cards. They had neat piles on their desks. They picked up a report card, wrote something on it and quickly moved it onto another pile.

Josh hoped that maybe he could get a blank one just to mess with.

Your son is really stupid. Have you thought of a special school?

We don't have the facilities here. Please make certain he bathes before class. His raunchy stench is disruptive.

His father had this whole other system. They had to move in a long collapsible table from the art room. Chick laid out all the report cards side by side. Everything had to be made into a Twister mat.

In the staff room there was a Coke machine. An old music teacher bought him a Five Alive. It was the first time he ever drank one. It was an awful thing to drink when you were looking at a Coke machine.

A pretty young teacher named Jill was moving cushions and looking under chairs.

"Chick, have you seen my agenda?" Jill asked.

"Why would I want your agenda?"

Everyone in the room got very quiet.

"I got my own agenda."

Josh knew he had no chance with Jill now.

At home in the kitchen, Chick explained the story to Frieda. He said Jill had been giving him the needles all week and he finally let her have it.

"The last thing someone wants to do is fall into my mouth," he said.

When she began to feel like there wasn't much time, Frieda started taking Chick on tours of the kitchen.

Chick used to go into the fridge whenever he needed sandwich bags. He would eat whatever was inside the bags and then use them to store cuff links.

Frieda was smiling.

"This is the cutlery drawer," she said, and Chick began to cry.

HE SAT at the bright yellow kitchen table. When he was drunk he always wanted to put his head down. And after that, the night was never any good.

It was like he was getting drunk and gearing up his whole life to write this one thing and he would need curtains to rip off the wall while he was doing it.

He was wearing the shirt that made him feel burly.

It all started after he had worn it to a lawn party and someone had taken a picture of him. He had looked at himself and thought, *boy, I sure can be a burly sonofabitch when I want to be.* But he never did look burly. There was only that one time. Maybe something was wrong with the film. Maybe there was some kind of eclipse that day. How could he have been so stupid? If he was close enough with someone to have told them that he thought the shirt made him look burly and that person threw it back at him in front of a whole bunch of people, he would scream, "That's such a lie! What a stupid thing to say! That's the stupidest thing I've ever heard you say!"

People would know something was up.

Her name was Talia and she was in from Israel with her family. She was staying with Josh's neighbors. She couldn't speak a word of English and Josh couldn't speak Hebrew, but it was the summer that *Grease* came out and he invited her and her younger sister over to their house to listen to the soundtrack while he danced for them.

He would fall down dead at the end of each song like he had just given them his all, but he'd always get up for the next one and they would laugh.

Before Talia went back to Israel, he gave her ten *Archie Digests*. He stacked them so all the spines lined up perfectly. He wanted them to look solemn and substantial, like a package wrapped in string from the old country.

"It's how I feel about you," he had wanted to say.

He always wanted to say that to somebody some day. He would tell them about the *Archie Digests* and say, "I always wanted to say it and I am finally saying it and it is to you."

He twiddled it in the back seat, his coat over his lap.

"You and your cousin decide on a pizza together," said his mother from the front. "You either share like normal people or we're going home."

"Talia's a stick in the mud," Frieda said.

"I thought you liked her," Josh said.

"What's to like?"

Josh imagined Talia as a poor old broken stick just stuck there in a big pit of mud. And there he was, trying his best to pull her out.

I MUST sit beside her, he thought. *She might like me. She might find me not so bad.*

Mara was friends with his neighbor. She remembered Josh from the time she was playing Chinese checkers on the front porch and his father was giving him a haircut on the driveway. Frieda was shouting directions from out the bedroom window.

"Your mom's pretty high-strung," she said.

"Joshua, you'd better clean your room," said Frieda. "It's disgusting."

"I like it like this. It's cozy."

"It looks like a crazy person lives here."

"Maybe one does."

"At least clean the dishes and put them away. I get depressed looking at them."

You are so beautiful, he thought.

Mara looked out the window of the school bus. The way her hands twisted in her lap made his heart break. *After school, those are the fingers that pull fried chicken from the basket.*

"So, what's your favorite song?"

"Probably something by the Beatles," said Mara.

When he went home he listened to his parents' copy of *Rubber Soul.* He lay on the carpet, the big brown earphones squished into the sides of his head. He stared at his dad's high school diploma on the wall and thought about Mara when she was a little girl dancing to "Michelle." Her parents must have loved her very much.

"Do you remember when I was a kid and you'd buy those steaks on a stick and you'd call them *lollies*? How the hell is a steak anything like a lollipop?"

"It was on a lollipop stick," Frieda said, "and you used to lick and lick them. You used to eat carrots like corn on the cob. You said it was how the kung fu experts did it."

After dinner, Joshua looked up Mara's name in the phone book. Her father's name was Jack.

"Hello."

"Hi. It's Josh."

"Hey."

"There's a documentary on Paul McCartney tonight. I thought you might want to see it."

"We don't get cable."

"I could tape it for you."

"We don't have a VCR."

"Ah."

"It doesn't matter. He isn't that hot a Beatle anyway."

"Who's your favorite?"

"Ringo."

"Why Ringo?"

"Because you can always see right into his nostrils."

He rubbed his feet back and forth on the library carpet and when she walked by, he touched her with the tip of his index finger.

IF YOU could jerk off to something else, like a hamburger, could you imagine the delight in being alive?

He was sure the Golden Age would have something of that to it.

When their parents went out, he slept over at Kaliotzakis's. They watched *The Love Boat* in his parents' bedroom, waiting anxious-fisted for the poolside scenes.

Kaliotzakis jerked with both hands, like he was rolling playdough into a thin hot dog.

They capped off the evening by pranking people in his mother's address book and eating TV dinners.

There was a story that Frieda always told. When she was a girl, her family had a country house and one time someone left the back screen door open. In the middle of the night, when she walked into the kitchen, she saw one of the walls covered in moths of all sizes.

"It looked like wallpaper", she said.

Fantasy: Mara sticks her hand into my rugby pants and flutters her hand around like a trapped bird. She goes, "Woo, woo," to make her friends laugh.

To try and analyze these things would be like ripping apart a colorful balloon to see what was inside that made it so colorful.

He was playing volleyball at the pool and the ball came down on the tip of his finger and pushed it out of joint. Tony, the head lifeguard, was playing backgammon with a bunch of girls. He tried to push it back to normal. When it just wouldn't go, Tony couldn't help but start to giggle, and so did the girls and so did Josh, just because he wanted to be a part of it all.

Josh went to the hospital and they had to set it and wrap it in gauze.

All summer, when he jerked off in the basement, he

would put his nose to the wrap and smell the medicinal odor. He didn't know what it reminded him of, it was just that it smelled so foreign from everything else around him: brisket, carpeting, laundry, onions. He began to think of it as the smell of some beautiful nurse lying in his arms.

All summer he snorted away at his mummified hand and thought about the women who were out there who didn't smell like anything he had ever imagined. He smelled that hand all summer long until it smelled just like himself and everything else in the house and it really didn't do a thing for him one way or the other.

There came a point when there wasn't anything you could say. All you could do was rub Frieda's legs.

WHEN THEY tried to gross each other out, Josh talked about the day he found Kaliotzakis's mother in the backyard raking leaves in her underwear.

"Her ass was so damn cute," he said.

Kaliotzakis talked about Josh's aunt Betty. She had a mole on her cheek the size of a grapefruit and Kaliotzakis went on about how wild she got when he gnawed on it.

"I once bought her a nipple tassel for it and taught her to spin it clockwise *and* counterclockwise. She's a talented old bird."

The day they kicked each other's asses in front of the library, the windows shook until the librarians ran outside screaming.

"I'll stick a bug so far up you," Kaliotzakis said as three cute librarians tore Josh's head out from his armpit.

In Josh's basement, they started inventing their own language. "Orange julep" was "unslep." "French fries" was "enchify." "Hot dog" was "otenhog." They only got three words into the whole thing.

Sometimes they'd lie in the basement at night and talk about what they'd do if they were downtown.

"I'd go up to some girl," Kaliotzakis said, "and I'd make her love me."

"What if all of this is a dream?" Josh said.

"I'm pretty sure it isn't," Kaliotzakis said.

He decided to go stay with Chick and Frieda.

"I'm not working now anyway," he said.

At the bus station he read magazines, his old canvas schoolbag packed with T-shirts and notebooks.

He kept expecting to see a little kid eating cotton candy.

He knew it would be enough to throw him over the edge.

The story was, Josh fainted at his own bris.

KALIOTZAKIS HAD this thing he did where he'd go up to people and ask them what time it was. All the while, his naked ass was popped out of his sweatpants so just Josh could see. There he'd be, having the most serious conversations, while Josh could see his ass right there on the street.

At the loser table, they ate egg salad out of Tupper-ware. At the popular table they ate cold-cut sand-wiches and drank soda. The popular table was in the corner, right beside the soft-ice-cream machine. When there was a birthday, they popped each other in the face with soft-ice-cream sandwiches. They had the whole machine to themselves.

He was riding on the bus back home to Chick and

Frieda. He looked at the back of the seat in front of him and he forgot what shirt he was wearing. He looked straight ahead and tried to see how long he could keep a thing like that forgotten.

The night before Frieda died, Chick spoon-fed her crushed ice. She kept taking away the spoon from him to feed herself and Chick thought everything was going to turn out fine.

He was coming up the staircase when he saw Chick on the landing. He looked up at his face and knew that Frieda was dead. He and his father had never looked at each other like that.

At the shiva, he did a magic trick for a little boy and everybody watched, smiling. Josh opened up his hand, one finger at a time, like petals blooming in time lapse. There was nothing in there.

"There's ten thousand dollars' worth of mirrors in this room," Josh said.

Kaliotzakis showed up at the shiva with his mother.

Kaliotzakis used to have thick long hair. Josh would brush it up and out until his head looked like a pompom. Josh said it was the latest style. He called it "The Beethoven."

Now Kaliotzakis was balding with a small scar on his forehead. He drove a cab and when he said "but um," he pronounced the "t" very hard.

Kaliotzakis told Josh about the woman from the

night before who got into his taxi with an open umbrella. She had milky, pale blue eyes and when he took a fast corner, he heard her head hit the door and her eyes in the rearview mirror didn't blink.

"The inside of my cab still smells like shepherd's pie," he said.

Reggie made him feel like he was nine years old and out for dinner with his family at the Ponderosa Steak House and he had run into his French teacher and his mother invited her to dine with them.

Reggie made him feel like he was sitting in a public bathroom stall and someone had come into the bathroom and began singing a song about what a stinky bastard he was while he was in there sweating it out.

Reggie made him feel like someone had taken the red Tonka fire engine he had always wanted and painfully corkscrewed it down the front of his jeans.

Reggie made him feel like the ice-cream man had just rolled by and all his dead grandparents were mooning him out the truck window.

Josh had these yellow notebooks and on each page there was a new idea for a TV script. Nothing was ever finished but the new ideas just kept coming. He started scripts about women who owned snakes and men who took public transportation. In the evening they met up in snack bars and played dominoes while the studio audience watched for the "APPLAUSE" sign.

He opened up a desk drawer and pulled out a Kleenex box full of old notes from girls. He could never bring himself to throw them out. He unfolded one. It started, "Math class is sooooo boring. That's probably why I'm writing you . . . just kidding!"

What will be the things I leave behind?

At some point he would be old, and there would be a team of Russian dancers who would come to the old-age home. There would be one Russian hell-bent on making Josh smile. He would kick his legs like a wild man, coming at Josh like all that kicking was to say, "Here is life! I am life!"

Josh would watch him plough across the floor, getting closer and closer, and he would feel a lifetime of hard-boiled eggs come up on him.

You weren't supposed to ring the door at a shiva house. You were supposed to just walk in.

Standing in the hallway in a long black coat was the rabbi. Josh hadn't seen him in years. His beard had gotten all white and his eyes looked like they had been soaking in Vaseline.

Chick got up to give him his chair. The rabbi said that this wasn't a time to be a good host; it was a time to mourn.

"It's just how I am," said Chick.

The rabbi asked Josh if he was planning to say kaddish.

Josh felt like saying something to him along the lines of "no hard feelings."

Sharing a locker with Vered in tenth grade was one of the luckiest things ever to happen to him. Just knowing that, no matter what, their boots were alone in the dark for six hours a day was enough to make him feel like at least something in his life was going right.

The first time he ever phoned her up, he was lying on his stomach on his parents' bed. He had his hand inside the front of his pants. He was watching himself in the dresser mirror. It was about locker business, about how he was wondering if she had seen this watch-pen of his. When he had the poison-control sticker just about peeled off the receiver, he launched into a long speech about the Three Stooges and how she should definitely check out their stuff. Then he asked her out.

They went to see the Eurythmics at this outdoor concert. He didn't know where he came up with the idea, but he wanted to hold her from behind and sway with her to the music. He knew that if he didn't do it he would hate himself.

Vered's friend Deborah was driving and they had to stop in the city to pick up her boyfriend. At his apartment, he opened the door in a bath towel. Josh had never seen a boy that hairy. He looked like he was about forty-five. In the car on the way to the show, he handed Josh a piece of licorice candy that almost burned a hole through his tongue.

During a slow song, Josh snuck up behind Vered and put his hands on her hips. He tried to ease them both into some kind of groove, but he only ended up almost ripping off her sneakers. For the rest of the evening, she was afraid to be near him. Deborah's boyfriend held them both, dancing with them in perfect unison like they were his back-up singers.

At home that night Josh ate a bowl of cereal while staring at a bottle of nail polish. Carefully, he painted his nails.

In bed, his fingers spider-walked the length of his ribs.

Quit tickling me. I have a plane to catch in the morning.

Josh was swimming. Using the palms of his hands, he pulled himself along the wooden floor of Vered's bedroom on his stomach. Her bed was the lifeboat. She was sitting up, reading a book. He begged her to pull him aboard. After a lot of begging and drowning, she offered him a foot. He grabbed hold of it.

"What's my foot's name?" she asked.

"Maureen," Josh answered.

She giggled.

"My hair," she said.

"Priscilla."

"My nose."

"Mumtaz the Magnificent."

"My breasts."

"Dolores and Delilah."

"My eyes."

"Sinclair. They both are."

"My ass."

"Henry."

"My right nipple."

"I'm not sure."

She pulled down the neck of her T-shirt and a little pink nipple poked out. It was like it used an independent personality to look Josh straight in the face. It cleared his sinuses with a sharpness that almost made his nose bleed.

"J.R.," he whispered.

After the crowd thinned out, Josh and the rabbi sat in

the kitchen. The rabbi picked at the crumbs on the table while he spoke. Josh wondered if it was a move rabbis picked up in rabbinical college.

"Do you still have your tephillin?" the rabbi asked.

"Somewhere."

"Come tomorrow and say kaddish. It will make your mother's journey easier."

The thought of Frieda on a *journey* was almost enough to make him giggly.

After the week of shiva was over, Josh went into the garage and poked around. He found the old Atari and hooked it up. He turned off all the lights in the basement and sat on the floor. Chick was sleeping on the couch, a book open on his chest. The TV screen looked like a Miró.

In the morning he called his landlord and told him he wasn't coming back. He couldn't live in a place that had mice.

In the theater her mouth moved warm and sure right over you. In the darkness, while she worked, you thought you were making eye contact with some guy.

You felt sorry for him.

When Kaliotzakis wasn't driving his cab, he worked at the Burger Zoo. He told Josh he could get him in.

At the interview, the manager took Josh to a windowless little room in the back. There was a telephone on the wall and a microwave on the counter. The manager leaned against the wall and crossed his arms. He was wearing a brown and orange striped shirt and his cap was brown. Everyone else wore an orange cap.

"Two things," said the manager. "One, I want a man who is willing to work. If you think you're going to come in here and eat fries and pick your ass all day, try again. People show up here and they're like, 'Yeah, the Burger Zoo. The Burger Zoo is cool, I could hang at the Zoo.' Well, if that's your attitude, the door's over there. Is that your attitude?"

Josh felt like his fingers were being skinned like carrots.

"Second thing I need to know is whether you're a winner or a loser, because I don't want losers on my team. Are you a winner or a loser?"

There was something about the way Vered danced that scared the crap out of him. It was like she was squishing out a cigarette with her foot. Over and over. He never understood that side of her. All her moves were straight from the cunt.

There was this kid with terrible acne who came into the Burger Zoo. His friends called him Howie. He was holding a bottle of ketchup and a big opened bag of ketchup chips. He ordered two hamburgers.

"With nothing on them," he said.

There was all this red crap around the rim of the ketchup bottle.

There's just no name for stuff like that, he thought.

"If I was Jesus," Kaliotzakis said, "my mother would have scratched a Roman's face. When they put the first nail in my hand, she would have gone ballistic. She would have screamed, 'No, no.' It would have been too much. Somebody would have had to kill her."

He began thinking about salvation all the time, and how it would go on forever and ever. It seemed as awful as death. He couldn't sleep at night. He alternated between sitting on the toilet and lying in bed with the lights on. At school he had tried to explain the situation of going on forever but nobody understood. He didn't try too hard because he didn't want to depress anyone and he still didn't understand it exactly.

The first thing he did after he moved back home was clean out the big freezer in the basement. Inside he found ice-cream containers filled with blocks of spaghetti sauce.

Pretty soon I'll never be able to eat her sauce again.

H E FOUND a paper in his old desk drawer with every-thing about Vered he could remember:

1. Her nose like a turtle.
2. Her twisted-up tights in the glove compartment of the car.
3. Her sweet-talking cab drivers for a few extra blocks.
4. Her wetting herself with drunken laughter.
5. The stories with no point.
6. The way the wind always lifted her skirt up over her waist, no matter how unwindy it was.
7. The way she'd say she'd call and wouldn't.
8. The way she got turned off by the least show of emotion.
9. The way she never knew how hard money was to come by.
10. The way she was so formal whenever she wrote a letter.

11. How she always wrote "Hollywood" over and over when she was doodling in her chemistry notebook.

12. How the first time I was at her house she made a big bowl of meat sauce and a tall glass of milk and didn't offer me any.

13. How she was so hairy and sometimes when she wore a dress it was like a caveman trying to fit in.

14. How she was so good at Ping-Pong because her folks had such a big basement.

15. How she'd lick my hands right after I fingered her.

The first time he ever met the rabbi was at Kaliotzakis's house. Kaliotzakis's parents were out and Josh and Kaliotzakis were lying in their king-size bed. It was summer, and their bedroom was the only air-conditioned room in the house. They were watching a show with dancing teenagers and Kaliotzakis was saying how he would fuck any one of those girls, when the doorbell rang.

Josh watched from the bedroom as Kaliotzakis opened the front door. There was a young man with a beard standing there smiling.

"I'm the new rabbi," said the man.

"Okay," said Kaliotzakis.

"We're building a synagogue at the end of your block. We're expecting to be able to start services by the end of the month and I was hoping we might be able to lure you boys over." The rabbi smiled broadly.

"Josh," Kaliotzakis called.

Josh came over and stood beside Kaliotzakis.

"I've come here all the way from the other side of the world," said the Rabbi. "I've come here because the Great Rebbe told me to, and when the Great Rebbe tells you to do something, you do it. So, here I am."

"Who's this Great Rabbi?" asked Kaliotzakis.

"He's a very great man. He has a lot to teach the world. You'll come by the shul and we'll make l'chaim."

He looked at the dental floss floating in the toilet bowl. It cast a shadow against the bottom. Things could get as insignificant as that. It was all a part of God's master plan.

WHEN VERED CALLED, Josh left right off the bat. Her house was four blocks away and he cycled over on pure ball steam. She was eating limp fries on her front porch. She made it look exotic. She kept pouring salt all over the plate.

"I'm gonna die from salt," she said.

In her room, she said she might as well show him her tits because she already showed them to her brother-in-law. She was wearing a brown sweatshirt that she lifted up two times, really fast.

She put on music and sat on his lap in front of the mirror.

"Let's see what we look like together," she said.

Vered gave him a piece of gum from her purse. It was so sour that he squinted. She said he looked like he was having an orgasm.

On Monday, in art class, he watched the teacher talk about how much he loved his nana and how sad he was now that his nana was dead. Vered was sitting on the table facing him, flashing her panties until the word "nana" sounded like the stupidest thing in the world.

He rode his bicycle home after his shift at the Zoo and stopped in every alley along the way. He looked through all the garbage until he found a little address book. He felt good to be alive when under "l" there was someone called Loco Amore.

Vered was the kind of girl who playfully sprayed herself with the garden hose during the dog days.

"Have you ever fantasized about me? Do you see me in short dresses, dancing to that shitty folk music you like? What color do you think my nipples are, red or pink?"

Up on the shelf in his old closet, there was a metal candy container. In it, there was a picture of Kay at the age of four. She was sitting on Santa's lap. She was dressed like a cowgirl and she had a gun pressed up against his bulbous nose.

Josh decided to say kaddish. He tried to get Kaliotzakis to come with him. "You could use a little religion," said Josh.

"I could use a piece of ass," said Kaliotzakis.

They sat in the back of the synagogue.

"It smells of old man in here," said Kaliotzakis.

Josh started to giggle.

Kaliotzakis let loose a fart.

Josh started laughing so hard he thought he would never stop.

One night while Chick was in the basement watching videos, Josh looked through Frieda's night table and found his baby book. Frieda had kept it even into his twenties. Scotch-taped to the first page was a flat cigar wrapped in plastic. There was a red sticker on it that said "It's a boy!"

He went out for a coffee and made sure he was completely spread out in the booth before he unwrapped it. He sucked at it until the girl who worked there told him to stop.

KAY CAME TROTTING down the stairs into the base-ment. She was in her underwear and he was playing video games, his philosophy textbooks spread out all over the floor. He watched her, the sound of men dying in the background.

What is it about legs? Or what is it about breasts? Or the small of a back? What is it about anything? One day there will be no difference between anything. It'll all be the exact same thing. One day you'll look in the dictionary and there will be only one word and you'll just have to make do.

In his old desk he found notes for a telephone conver-sation with Kay:

— glad you caught her.
— sounding effervescent as always (joke).
— how was your summer?

Only if things are going well:

— I think about you a lot—the stuff about the little girl on the boardwalk, candy apple, bag of Cheezies.
— just want to see your face—miss seeing it.
— you were the best thing that ever happened to me.

"Oh, there is definitely something wrong with my uncle Rupert," Kay said. "He asked if I had ever heard of the joy-buzzer tampon and then he stuck his finger in my crotch and vibrated it. I laughed just because I didn't want him to feel bad. Dad says he's really insecure and vulnerable since his divorce."

"What a horrible humiliation," Josh said. "To get your

dog fucked! If you really want to show a man who's boss, you fuck his dog, plain and simple—and you try to make the dog really like it."

"Remember when the Six Million Dollar Man had to push the moon back into orbit?"

They were in the basement. He hit *play*.

Kay settled into this position on the couch. Her ass was perfectly pressed against the back of his forearm. He kept his arm there, as nervous and still as a hummingbird. He had never been as happy on that couch as he was right then.

The images on the screen were sunk in pea soup.

That night he dreamt they attacked each other on the street, ripping each other's clothes off while people in restaurant windows watched.

"LENNY BRUCE SAID that and Lenny Bruce said this," he was saying.

Lenny Bruce was king of the Jews and Josh was trying to impress Kay. She was on her way to an art history class. She said he should come over for fish sticks some time. She was wearing a green leotard. He couldn't believe it.

He said things like, "My mother's food, häh! Are you kidding . . . Uncle Shlepsy almost . . . The ice-cream man doesn't stop in front of our house any more . . . my father, a wild man: 'Where's the car keys? Who left the stereo on?'"

"Jewish men can be really sexy," she said.

They went out to the Chinese buffet and Chick piled mountains of food on his plate. Josh used to call that "Flintstone-sized portions." When one would get up to go get food the other one would just be starting into his plate. That was the way it turned out. They were hardly sitting together at all.

"Everything here tastes like urine," said Chick, "leather and urine."

"It's funny how when you're at a Chinese buffet," said Josh, "all you end up talking about is the buffet."

Chick used to call mucus *goojoo*. It was dripping out of him like he was a cracked egg about to lose his yolk.

"I love you, I love you," he kept saying.

Everything would get funnier as he got older. He figured by the time he reached his deathbed, he'd be in stitches around the clock.

"I used to be a very handsome man," he would say, "and I had an excellent head for figures."

"That's good," the nurse would say.

"Life is quick," he would whisper. "It's a fucking dream."

HER FAMILY WENT on a bus tour when Kay was five years old. The whole bus played bingo. At the front, Kay read out numbers into a microphone. She read the numbers off the balls as someone handed them to her. She read each number twice. She sounded like a child star.

The bus driver was smiling. He tried to tell her a joke.

"Shut up and keep your eyes on the road," she said.

Frieda and Chick had gone to the Poconos for the weekend so they took over their bedroom. Josh moved in the stereo. They listened to the Clash and moved things from the freezer into the microwave. They made love for the first time. Afterwards, Kay lay beside him and cried.

"Do you want me to sleep on the floor?" he asked.

"That would only make it worse," she said.

It was Kay's idea to move his parents' bed over to the window. In the morning, he rolled over and looked outside. There wasn't a cloud in the sky. The red brick building across the street looked like the most real thing in the world. He thought of waking her so she could see, but he didn't know what it was he wanted her to see.

You will never forget this, he thought.

One night he dreamt that she was talking on a pay phone in the rec center and he pulled down her pants. Her anus was perfectly hairless and pink. It smelled like shampoo. She cupped the receiver, whispering something.

"CHICK, bring up the soda from the basement," said Frieda, stirring a pot of cabbage soup.

"Nectar was always a big treat in our house," said Kay. She was trying hard, playing with the strings on her pants.

He knew Frieda wasn't ever going to like Kay so he figured he might as well have fun.

He put his hand in the back of Kay's pants.

Her ass was cold and refreshing.

On TV, King Kong Bundy holds a wrestler's head in a submission hold. The tattooed forearm of the referee reaches out towards Bundy's shoulder. The head in Bundy's hands looks like Jesus on the cross but without the dignity or love. King Kong Bundy, all 440 pounds of him, is smiling into the camera. Josh tries to imagine what it's like to be his mother.

The rabbi convinced Josh and Kaliotzakis to form a discussion group with him. They would meet on Tuesday nights after Josh's shift at the Burger Zoo. The first night the three of them sat around the rabbi's dining room table and drank ginger ale and ate wafer cookies.

"When the Rebbe was five years old," said the rabbi, "he saw his father was about to kill the family dog because it had eaten a chicken from the yard and in those days if, God forbid, you lost a chicken, maybe you wouldn't eat for a week, so it was a very horrible thing. The father was holding the axe handle over the dog's head, about to bring it down and end the poor mutt's life, when the Rebbe said, 'Tateh, if you kill the dog you might be killing the Rebbe Nachman of Chelm who wanted to be reborn a dog.' So his father, a pious man in his own right, decided to spare the dog's life. And from that day on, the father would only refer to the dog as Rebbe."

"So he scammed his dad," said Kaliotzakis.

"The Rebbe knew that the dog was really a great scholar."

"How could he know that?" asked Kaliotzakis.

"Because he's the Rebbe," said the rabbi.

"But the dog's also the Rebbe."

"The dog was only *a* rebbe. The Rebbe was *the* Rebbe."

"That's fucked up," said Kaliotzakis.

Josh sat there feeling sorry for the rabbi.

He wrote in his notebook: *Everything in life, and I mean everything, is white feathers and snow. Even pain is. But Kay's red panties are a scythe.*

"DID YOU SEE the matzo ball your mom gave me?" asked Kay. "It wasn't even a ball."

There was a handyman in their old building who once stuck a screwdriver under a woman's skirt in the elevator. He didn't touch her with it or anything. He just kept it under her skirt. His name was Joe and he was drunk most of the time. They fired him after that.

Every so often Josh thought about looking him up. He saw himself going into Joe's apartment, the whole place smelling like Campbell's Tomato Soup and Vicks VapoRub.

Joe would sit him down on this couch all covered in blankets. There would be crooked bullfighting paintings on the wall, washed-out soup cans full of pens and pencils, rubber bands around the door knobs—that sort of thing. Joe would bring him out a cup of instant coffee in a mug that said "Gemini" with wide-eyed little twins. He would put it down on the TV tray and it would sound like a toy snare drum.

Josh would wait for the right pause. He would tilt his head a little and look at him until Joe knew why. He would say, "She was my mother."

But then he would laugh.

In the dream I was in this religion where everyone prayed to this awful woman who made them bite her toes. She made them read to her and when she would start to fall asleep, they would stop, but then she would wake up and say, "Keep reading, I'm not asleep yet." In the beginning they liked reading to her. In the beginning it was something that they thought was nice. They were flattered, in a way. Do you see what I'm getting at here?

Josh and the new guy were the only ones on the floor. The new guy was practicing kung fu moves over by the fryer, lost in his own little world.

"My uncle touched my ass once," Kay said. She was drunk and talking to the night watchman. "Everyone was in the other room. He slung me over his lap and pulled my pants down. His living room was real plush— candy dishes full of toffee, thick carpeting. Everyone was in the kitchen eating roly-polies and looking at wedding pictures. I was laughing my head off."

Rip Taylor was running through the audience of the *Mike Douglas Show* throwing confetti when a man jumped up and started yelling at him about what an awful dad he had always been and why was he acting like such a big shot on TV when he didn't give a shit about his own son.

But Rip Taylor kept on throwing confetti, even harder maybe, and the music kept going. When they came back from the commercial nobody said a thing.

He wrote to the chip company. His letter contained a recipe that involved soaking chips in milk for an hour and then serving them in a bowl and eating them with a spoon like cereal.

"An after-school treat," he wrote. They sent him three free coupons and told him that his letter was up on a special bulletin board. He wondered what it looked like up there.

He loved the feeling of creaming onto her ass. It was all over, it always felt like. Everything was completely over and done with. After he creamed her ass, he just wanted to be thrown into an open grave. He didn't want to just go to bed. That wasn't what this was about at all.

K AY'S FATHER SAT outside on the patio and looked at the papers on the kitchen table. He had wanted to name Kay *Anna*. His wife wouldn't let him because she'd once worked with someone named Anna and she would never be able to get that woman's face out of her mind.

"Anna," he said.

Kay imitated his mother. She put the throw cushions from the couch in her pants to make her ass real big. She picked things off the coffee table and looked at them trying like crazy not to laugh.

"Oh, these are nice," she said, "but Barney's mother can get you the same ones for next to nothing."

Later on, he was getting light-headed. He was snorting those cushions so hard his brain popped.

The next time they had their discussion group, Kaliotzakis stayed home. Josh and the rabbi met in the basement of the synagogue. The rabbi sat at the other end of the table and played with his beard.

"How do we know anything is real?" asked the rabbi.

"We don't," answered the rabbi. "We don't know anything whatsoever. You don't even know if you're sitting here. We're all floating in a jar of formaldehyde," said the rabbi, "and only the Rebbe can unscrew the cap."

HE WATCHED her while she slept and pretended she was dead. He'd go at it until his cheeks were shiny with tears.

"Sex doesn't turn me on any more," Kay's father said. "I don't know what I live for."

He looked at his daughter like she knew something. After all, she came out of him.

They had just finished eating the sushi she had made and they were lying on his bed. They were very happy.

"I want you to meet my mother," she said.

She called her up in Europe and held the phone so that Josh could hear, too.

Her mother told amusing anecdotes in a light British accent. There was never a point to anything

Josh's mother said. Frieda's stories usually ended with, "and I bargained him down to half." Kay's mother's stories had buttons.

Kay said, "I'd like you to meet Joshua," and then she handed him the phone.

There was this joke he wanted to make. He should have written it down. There were long pauses after everything he said. The receiver was getting sweaty. He was making conversation and she was making pauses.

She was trying very hard to hear something in his voice. He couldn't control all those terrible things that kept coming out of him.

There was a man who ordered a vanilla milkshake in the Burger Zoo at the end of Josh's shift. He was small and skinny and it was after midnight and that was all he ordered. Just the shake.

The man went back to his table, pulled an oversized calculator out of a crumpled plastic bag and started punching buttons. He went back to the counter.

"You charged me too much tax," he said to the girl.

She called Bob the manager over. No one knew what the man was talking about. He went back to his seat and punched buttons on the calculator like he was dialing an ambulance, a piece of finger on the bathroom floor. He looked over at Josh.

"I'll pay fifteen percent with a smile."

Kay made this friend at school. His name was Reggie and he was also a writer.

Josh said that he knew a guy named Reggie.

Kay said that Reggie knew him, too.

She said Reggie once peed beside Leonard Cohen in the bathroom at Ben's Delicatessen. Josh began giving every guy beside him at the urinal the once-over. He was starting to think of himself as plain ordinary.

"He's a very fine poet," she said. "He writes with a quill on rice paper."

She told him that he could never hang out with Reggie because Reggie was very particular about who he talked to. Then she started saying things like, "I told Reggie what you said to me and he said that if he was there he would have punched you in the nose."

So one day he went to meet Kay after school to see her with Reggie. He waited at the gates of the campus. He worked a Mr. Freeze, casual-like.

As they walked toward him, Kay was laughing, flinging her long blonde hair around like she owned the joint. Reggie was making points, his hands out and wagging, his eyebrows lifted high up as though to say, isn't life the way I describe it a strange yet beautiful trip?

That Mr. Freeze was sucking something out of him.

"Hey," Josh said.

He caught her eye and she looked at him the way she looked at other people when she was with him.

"So why don't you punch me in the nose?" he asked as Reggie's shaking hand just hung there.

"You are such an asshole," said Kay.

"I wanna be an asshole," he said.

What if she were a lifeguard when you were a kid at the top of the high diving board? Would she blow her whistle at you until you forgot how to dive?

CHICK HAD BEGUN to wear his hair slicked back. It was something Frieda could never stand, but now it didn't matter. It made Chick look older. Sometimes late at night Josh heard the sound of hairspray coming from out of the bathroom. It came out in a long hiss. Sometimes it lasted for minutes.

The moustache that he thought would be charming was cheesy. Not only that, but he believed it was making his feet stink worse.

He was writing a script about a private dick named Luco who has a passion for jerking off. The way other film noir types drank in bars between fistfights and stakeouts, this guy would masturbate. During the opening credits, there would be a close-up of his face coming behind the wheel of his car, his shoulders moving up and down and Lou Reed's "Sweet Jane" playing.

"Who's going to watch a movie like that?" Kay asked.

"Angry little pubescent boys," Kay answered herself.

As she walked through the arch onto the campus, Josh wanted to run her over.

"What the hell did you do to the steering wheel?" Frieda asked.

I would still have sex with you even if you were sixty. I would do it if you were eighty. Even if you were only twelve. I would have sex with you even if you had a penis. I would let you shove it in me. I would yelp. I would stare at the wall and yelp.

Kay had pudgy Flintstone feet.

He watched her eyelids while she slept. She was wearing a miniskirt. He watched her in the grass, too nervous to sleep because of the ants. They were surrounded by beer bottles and opened cheeses. He looked up at the top of the trees and the sky. It was very simple up there.

"Reggie's so sensual", she said. "In the winter he slithers down the sidewalk on his stomach. Everyone dies of laughter."

On the subway they didn't speak a word. A guy in a cowboy hat asked her for directions.

She was drifting over the buildings. She was a pink Chagall cow. He was a neurotic Jewish rooster pecking at her foot.

THE PICKLES he bought were the wrong kind of pickles. He wanted the crunchy kosher kind that made you feel like you were biting your boss's prick off, the kind of pickle that made a crunch that could punctuate a call to arms. The pickles he bought were yellowish and slimy and sweet. It was what his mother called "a real goyish pickle."

He looked down at the sandwich on his plate and slowly pressed his fist into the bread until smoked meat spit out the sides.

Take that, you Nazi bastards.

He kept saying I and inventing new I's to say I with. It was like those Russian dolls. He was getting further and further away from something and closer and closer to nothing.

At the old-age home, there would come a point where he would have no appetite any more. Everything would taste like Silly Putty. His throat would feel like an elevator shaft made of Melba toast.

One morning he would get an idea.

"Everything tastes better on a wooden ice-cream paddle," he would say. "Get me one of those and then we're in business."

He would tell three nurses. He would tell an orderly. He would tell a doctor. Eventually he would just shut up.

"Your laugh is like a mouse running out of your pant leg. When I first met you, I wanted to make you laugh until you cried," Josh said.

"You just skipped the laughing part," Kay said.

"I didn't say you were a fucking idiot," Josh said. "I said you were *like* a fucking idiot."

Kay was cleaning out his room of all her things. She was a methodical blonde Zamboni.

After she left he saw a shimmering ring of celestial light in the middle of the double parlor, and when he stepped through it he was in the bathroom of his childhood house. He was crying on the floor, pulling toilet paper off the spool with both hands like he was climbing a rope.

THE LAMP that bore his likeness was defective. It never worked properly. "Have your likeness immortalized as a lamp," the ad read. Have friends and family "turn you on." That piece of crap never worked right from day one.

Frieda went to Miami because her aunt had died. The first night she was gone, Chick decided to make hamburgers.

"In the army I cooked for hundreds of men," he said.

Chick used the oven timer. Josh had never seen Frieda use it once. For dessert Chick roasted a single marshmallow over the stove until the house was filled with smoke.

Script idea: *Mary Poppins* has just played on TV and all

the kids on this street start running around with umbrellas. The children go up to the roof and dare each other to jump. They think that if they jump off the roof with an umbrella they'll be okay. One kid gets stuck in a tree. Another kid lands on the hood of a car and breaks his leg. A reporter is sent to ask people on the street about the epidemic.

Sample dialogue (big truck-driver-looking guy): "I think it's just sickening. They ought to be more careful with what they put on the TV. There's kids out there for shit's sake."

His name was Barry and he was with his wife and kid. Josh ran into them at the home show. Barry was looking for a good kitchen surface for their new place. Josh had just wandered in off the street because he was looking for a warm place to eat the sandwiches in his pocket.

He ran into Barry in front of a display of blenders.

"I heard about your mother," said Barry, and he seemed to mean it.

They talked and the kid played with a blender,

clicking it on and off. Barry's wife nodded her head a lot. Before they parted, Barry hugged him tightly.

Those sandwiches looked like hell after.

"I'd like a girlfriend with a limp," he said.

AFTER Frieda was gone, Chick would use the barbecue to cook all his meals. It was like he just couldn't go in the kitchen. Sometimes he would start grilling hamburgers at four in the morning. He would silently turn them over the grill with his head tilted like he had just forgotten what he was going to say.

They sat in the synagogue basement and the rabbi told him about the time he met the Rebbe in Atlantic City when he was a boy. The Rebbe had told him that he would have to move halfway across the world in order to do his work.

"This was at a time when the Rebbe didn't have as many followers," he said. "You could actually have a sit-down with him."

The rabbi slammed the table with the palm of his hand as he said this.

"The Rebbe is a five-star general in the army of God, and we're just privates. The Rebbe has told us that redemption is about to happen. Every moment the Moschiach is not revealed means there is a greater likelihood he will be revealed in the next moment. And we believe that the Rebbe *is* the Moschiach. Our heart breaks with every second we have to spend in exile."

It would be awful if there was a bully and the bully made me take off my clothes. It would be just terrible if this was on the street where a little girl could see me and ask her father if I was the same kind of monkey that Tarzan had in the cartoons.

"LOVE, Kay," it says at the end of the letter, but it's written on top of Liquid Paper. He only notices the Liquid Paper later, after he has read the letter several times. He holds the letter up to the light and sees through the Liquid Paper the words "Rock on." She has never used an expression like that before, not even ironically.

Then one day she calls him up and leaves a message on his answering machine.

"I'll be home at eight," she says. "No wait, I'm lying. I won't be home until nine." *No, wait, I'm lying?* What the hell is going on here?

Two weeks later he is sitting on a park bench with Kaliotzakis. All the way down the street he sees Kay. She is with a man. As they get closer and closer he tries to decide what the first thing he will say should be. Kaliotzakis is a kidder. Josh isn't in the mood to be kidded.

When they are several feet away he realizes that Kay is with his father. He forgets what he is going to say.

They just keep walking. Neither Kay nor his father look at him. It isn't like they're pretending or anything. It's like they really don't know him.

Later on, just as he's going to bed, the phone rings. It's Kay. She's asking for Theodore.

"Theodore speaking," he says.

He goes right along with it.

It is as though, being raised on a farm, Reggie often had to spank the pigs to tenderize their bacon.

His laugh is so smug and invincible, it's like he has a pipe clenched between his teeth during the opening song of his own Christmas special.

When Frieda used to make dinner there were a million and one side orders. Now, when his father grilled a steak, it was just the steak. Sometimes he would put some baked beans in a bowl at the center of the table.

That bowl of baked beans would look like the loneliest thing in the world.

He once read a book where things went on forever. That book was only 312 pages.

CHICK WENT down into the synagogue basement. The bulb had burned out so Josh and the rabbi were sitting at the table in the dark.

"What's going on down here?" asked Chick.

"The teachings of the Rebbe will illuminate even the darkest darkness," said the rabbi, smiling.

"I'm waiting outside with the engine running for almost twenty minutes," said Chick.

"You should come by on Thursday nights when we have the couples' class," said the rabbi.

In the car, Josh tried to explain why it all wasn't so weird.

"Who the hell sits around in the dark?" asked Chick.

Josh was lying on the living room couch with an activity book opened on his chest. Outside on the back porch, the barbecue was going. Chick was looking up into the sky with binoculars.

Kaliotzakis gave his cat a voice. It was a southern-belle sort of thing. He made his voice high-pitched. He talked to his little brother Richie in the voice and Richie would talk back to the cat. Just as Richie started to get into it, telling it about all the stuff that happens at school and even arguing with it, Kaliotzakis looked him straight in the eye. In his regular voice he said, "Why are you talking to a cat?"

If there is going to be a film about my life, there should be a scene where I fall off the couch in my sleep.

To keep cool I fill my belly button with water. It gives me a thimble of oasis.

Josh looked through her bathroom garbage. Mimi was cute and a good dancer. He looked through her garbage for anything. He didn't know what he was looking for. It wasn't like he had said, "I hope I find some toenail clippings." He didn't have a single idea. When he stuck his hand in there and moved it around in the toilet tissue and Q-Tips, he hadn't an idea what the hell he was looking for.

After Chick farted and Frieda got angry, he would sing, "I beg your pardon. I never promised you a rose garden."

Sometimes Chick would drop a roll of toilet paper

in the toilet. He would dry it out and still use it. No one else would. Frieda would say, "Don't use your father's toilet paper."

As Chick got older he started to drop the toilet paper into the toilet more and more often. It was as if he liked it that way.

Bob the manager made up this game where everyone had to work as fast as they could. He divided everyone at the Burger Zoo into two teams. One team was called Abba and the other was called the Beatles. Josh was on the Beatles.

Bob would stand there and clap his hands like a metronome, getting faster and faster. Douglas would make noises like he was going at warp speed and Bob would laugh.

Josh tried his best to get the sweat from his forehead to land right on the buns until Abba won.

After that day Bob started calling Josh "Yoko."

Mimi went to a high school with a swimming pool.

"You had to swim in gym class?" Josh asked.

"Yes," she said.

"You mean you had to get into a bathing suit and

get wet? What if you were hairy? What if you hated the cold?"

She didn't know. She didn't have those problems.

"There were these Korean kids," she said. "They always stayed in the shallow end. While we were learning water polo, they were popping their heads out of the shallow end, spraying water from their mouths and bouncing around. They always showed up wearing goggles and bathing caps."

He figured he would have just hung with the Koreans.

Shortly after he first arrived in town, the rabbi convinced Chick and Frieda to attend his discussion group for couples. Several weeks after, he called them up one night after midnight.

"There's going to be a very important announcement tonight," he said.

Frieda said that when a rabbi calls you, no matter what time it is, you get out of bed, so Chick put his pants on and said that he was sick and tired of the Jews telling him what to do.

At the rabbi's house, the rabbi's wife answered the door. She told them she was very sorry they were dragged out of bed like this.

In the background, the rabbi was on his knees pulling his beard in two directions and his in-laws were trying to put him to bed.

Earl: (*voice-over*) Audrey had one of those sexy popular-girl telephone numbers. It had three twos in a row. God gives the finest of the species the easiest numbers to remember. That is one of the many ways in which God proves himself to be such an unfair bastard.

    At home, I put the scrap with her number onto my bed and I am about to kiss it.

Mother walks in. She is going out for a night on the town with his father.

Mother: There's some fish sticks in the downstairs freezer. Eat them up and don't make me a million dishes.

Earl: (screaming his head off) Get out of my room!
Mother: Don't you open a mouth like that to me.

Earl calls Audrey up. They make a date. They go out that night to the rec center for some roller skating. They do the slow dances in the dark. He excuses himself and goes into the bathroom to jerk off in a stall. He looks through the window onto the alley and sees Audrey in her rented roller skates dancing seductively for a circle of older boys. He comes and leaves the bathroom.

CUT TO: Earl's mother and father are at a soirée. His mother has had a bad reaction to some fish and has spontaneous diarrhea. The father pulls out his hankie and makes it into a makeshift diaper for his wife. She puts it on in the bathroom so they do not have to end their evening early. In her stall, she looks out the window and in the reflection, sees her face, wrinkled and heavily made-up. She throws up in the toilet, gets her husband and they leave. When they get home they find Earl crying. The family dog has died.

END

He wanted all the air he would ever breathe to smell like her. Maybe the air he already breathed smelled like God. Maybe he had gotten so used to it from smelling it every day that it didn't smell like anything any more. It just smelled like air.

THEY BELIEVED that the man who would be the Moschiach was the Great Rebbe. He lived in New York and he had a long white beard. Every year, on his birthday, he got a letter from Jimmy Carter. There were stories of the things he had done. The Great Rebbe had remembered the middle name of someone he had met fifty years earlier.

They told him that the Moschiach was so close to coming that it could happen any second. It could happen even now, they said. Josh could feel in his bones exactly what they meant.

They were pounding the table and singing, "We want Moschiach now, we want Moschiach now, we want Moschiach now and we don't want to wait." Josh didn't want to do anything any more. He didn't see the point.

On the day the Great Rebbe died, his followers wandered the streets pulling their hair out and throwing themselves on the ground. There was a squad of specialists who came to work with them. They knew how to deal with this kind of thing.

Josh's favorite was when Mimi kissed him and jerked him off at the same time. It helped him feel the kiss the way it should be. Everything was often so dead but her hand was like a jumper cable.

HE TRIED TO FIT too much of her foot into his mouth. He felt himself start to gag. He hadn't thrown up in over ten years. If he was going to throw up he wanted it to happen outside an all-you-can-eat Chinese buffet. He wanted little Chinese boys and girls to scream in horror and delight.

He wondered what it felt like for her to have so much foot in there.

He woke up in the middle of the night and felt nothing but that he was alive. This was the panic he kept trying to describe. Being.

Cripes, Eddy, he would say to God, *I'm really over a barrel here.*

When I was nine my aunt took me to a Beach Boys concert.

When they started playing I kept looking and looking. I was freaked out because I thought the Beach Boys were supposed to be girls. I thought I was going to throw up. My aunt was laughing.

"They'd be called the Beach Girls," she said.

Then they threw beach balls into the audience. Everyone in the audience was trying like crazy to get a smack in. After a while, one came right at me. My aunt was going, "Get it! Get it!"

I was fed up.

There were even a couple of Beach Boys who had beards.

He applied the flesh-colored lipstick to the tip of his penis.

One time they were eating Chinese food and running out of things to say. She picked up his knuckle between two chopsticks and made like she was eating him up.

Josh liked doing it doggie-style because Mimi had an ass full of personality.

He wished he could put her head on the lower part of her back like Schroeder did with the bust of Beethoven on his piano.

She had a lovely face and he often got lonely back there without it.

Chick was in the basement. Josh was in Chick's bedroom, crawling around beside the bed, when he saw a little green bottle. He held it by the neck and it felt good there, like a hammer that meant business. He smelled the rim. It smelled of something fresh. It smelled like something hollow and oily, but very open and large. The label on the bottle read "The Rebbe's Kosher-style Love Lotion."

JOE PINCUS WAS a loud-mouth carpet salesman. At the synagogue, he was in charge of folding and unfolding bridge chairs on the high holidays.

One time in the coat check Pincus saw Josh doing an imitation of Charo. Kaliotzakis was grabbing Josh's nipples and yelling "Hoocheecoochee."

From that time on, Pincus figured Josh for some kind of kibitzer.

"You know who has nice tatas?" asked Pincus, approaching them in the darkness. "The rabbi's wife has nice tatas."

Josh watched Sophia Loren being interviewed on PBS. She sat in front of a black backdrop.

"My life is like a fairy tale," she said.

At one point, the interviewer asked her why she was smiling.

"I don't know," she said. She said it like a little girl, playing with her fingers. She was playing with her fingers on TV.

He thought of Kay. He imagined her saying "I don't know" when she was in her sixties. She would also say it like a little girl. He knew this. It made him sick that he knew this.

At the back of the synagogue, Pincus explained to Josh all about the Rebbe's Kosher-style Love Lotion.

"Love Lotion gave us our sense of community", said Pincus. "Life was sexier back then."

Josh thought of the green bottle under Chick's bed.

"So what happened to it?" asked Josh.

"What happened . . . I bet no one will tell you, eh? They won't tell you because it's *an embarrassment*. They'll only tell you the party line. They had to get it off the shelves because someone was threatening to reveal the secret ingredient."

"Which was what?" asked Josh.

"I'll tell you this much: it wasn't Thousand Island salad dressing. The Rebbe was a good man; he just wasn't perfect, no matter what they try to tell you. He went to the toilet just like everybody, fashtey?"

Script idea: At a party she calls him her wonky little bedfellow, so when they get home the first thing he does is pour a bowl of fruit cocktail onto the keys of her piano.

"How surreal," she says.

"I'll show you surreal," he says. So he pulls out a grapefruit from the fridge and pours vodka all over it. When it's good and doused, he pulls out his lighter and sets it on fire. Immediately, it falls from his hand and starts to burn into the carpet.

Panicking, he pulls out his prick and pisses all over the fire.

"Eep," he shrieks.

"Bravo," she says when his flow is finished. "Bravo."

"They're the same person."

"How can you say a thing like that?"

"They only have different-colored hair."

"I don't know what comic *you're* reading, but in the comic I read, Veronica is someone who really cares about her friends and doesn't exploit her wealth or power for personal gain. And Veronica has got some ass. Betty Cooper is a liar and a flat-ass."

"GIMME a french-fried potato," the old man said.

The deal with old people was that they never said "please." They spent the whole day at the Burger Zoo, eating their yogurt from home and stealing grocery bags full of napkins.

"Tell me", asked the old man, "why don't you make hard-boiled eggs for breakfast? They should drop dead with their sunny side up."

"I'm with you on that one," Josh said.

Old men looked awful with yolk dripping down their chins.

"Can you say something to them for me?" he asked.

"I could, but I doubt they'd care."

"Maybe you could boil a couple up for me once in a while?"

"We don't have any pots," he said.

"I could bring one of my own," the old man said.

Josh imagined holding the man's head in his lap and yelling at Bob the manager.

"Can't you see this man needs a goddamn hard-boiled egg?"

He humped her and thought about her surrender. When that was no longer enough, he said to himself, "It looks like Ms. Power Suit has been taken down a notch." After that he would close his eyes when he thrust, thinking about girls in his class from eleventh grade hobbling down the corridor with their pants around their ankles.

"I once met the Rebbe in the late seventies," said Pincus. "His people had rented out the whole roller-skating rink at the rec center. It was some affair."

"What was he like?" asked Josh.

"He's a very holy man," said Pincus, "but to be honest he's not exactly my cup of tea. I'll tell you who I did like, though: the Rebbe's brother Phil. Phil sang with the band and mixed these wonderful cocktails you could drop dead for. There's a guy I could have a good time with."

Josh was glad Mimi was wearing her pizza delivery cap. It made her look like the hot girl next door with plenty of Jackson Browne music. What she called "hat head," he found incredibly sexy. Her hair was so thick. She once convinced a little boy that it was transplanted from a horse's tail.

They walked to the gas station for smokes. It was after midnight and she kept wanting to stop and sit on the curb.

It was the first time he had worn the new Levi's from way in the back of his drawer. They fit him too loose. They were stiff and loose. It made him feel like a little kid playing dress-up with everyone walking in.

"Hey, Reggie," Mimi said. Reggie poked the gas nozzle into his Hyundai. He was flipping through his wallet like a man with a stacked liquor cabinet and a kitchen full of clean white appliances.

"Going, going, gone," said Reggie, pointing at Josh's hairline.

"You know Reggie?" she asked.

AN EXCERPT from a script in progress:

Chico: Betty, sweetheart, they whacked Sal. He did the saddest thing with his lips. They looked like cut-up caterpillars thinking *why me* in this big sad world. His eyes were like they were saying *take me*, like maybe they didn't have to go, like I could rush them to you in a cigar box, to let them see you one more time. He loved you, Betty. That I know. Winter is coming and we'll do what we can to help, but each of the seasons will be sad and hard in a new way without him around. He said he had something he wanted to give you and he kept pinching his stomach. I'll be damned if I could figure it out.

Kaliotzakis's little brother Richie was seven years old and a little slow. Richie sat in his room in his pajamas all day and listened to novelty records on his little record player. He would listen and chew on the cuffs of his pajama sleeves.

The greatest thing Kaliotzakis felt he knew how to do was this thing he did to Richie.

Kaliotzakis would walk into Richie's room and sit on the edge of his bed. He would watch Richie with a very serious look on his face. When Richie looked back, Kaliotzakis would sing:

Don't cry out loud,
Keep it inside,
Learn how to hide your feelings.

"But I'm not crying," Richie would say over and over. He would keep saying it until he started to cry. Kaliotzakis was then ready for the second part. He would sing while he pinched Richie's cheeks:

Baby face,
You've got the cutest little
Baby face.

That would really get Richie going, rolling across the carpet. He would look at the ceiling with his mouth open, panting, like there was a burning meatball on his tongue.

Josh wanted Richie to turn into this thing that he knew was possible. He didn't care if Richie had to die for it. He knew it was out there and Kaliotzakis was making it happen for them.

Chick and Frieda had routines, one of which was the this-coffee-tastes-like-dishrag-water routine. It went like this: Frieda would start by serving Chick a cup of instant coffee.

"This coffee tastes like dishrag water," Chick would say.

"Then don't drink it," Frieda would say.

Chick would ask everyone to smell it. Everyone would decline. He couldn't figure it out. Some days it tasted fine.

He was holding out a melted Three Musketeers bar but she was so cool and aloof, rolling her eyes and reading Simone de Beauvoir. *If I was Jean-Paul Sartre,* he thought, *I would stick my thumb in her ass and she would beg for more.*

She put down her book and asked him if she could look into his pee-hole.

"I let you look into me," she said.

When he was four, something had happened with hot Chinese mustard when he was naked and running around a coffee table. Now he pretended his pee-hole didn't exist.

She held it like a pirate telescope. His hands were sweaty. He slicked back his hair. "I love you very much," he said. She looked so serious. He wanted her to smile.

There was one time he waited in her bed over an hour, naked, just wearing his cowboy boots and reading an *Archie Digest*. The look on her face when she walked in, it hardly seemed worth the wait.

Certain things Reggie pulled on Archie made him horny. One time, lying in bed with his mother, he read a story where Reggie and Archie were stuck on a roof. They had to get down so Reggie told Archie to take off his pants so he could use them as a rope. On his way down they ripped, and Reggie just walked off. "So long sucker," he said.

"What do you see in there?" he asked.

Love Lotion was a light blue cream that came in a dark green glass bottle. The Rebbe was right there on the label giving the world the thumbs-up. The Rebbe looked like the kind of man who took no guff. Pincus told him that not only was the Rebbe a spiritual human being, but he was also strong enough to dangle a full-grown man from his beard.

"In his youth, he could roll a barrel of lotion with each hand," said Pincus. "That takes enormous strength."

Josh had never seen Pincus so impressed.

At the end of the night in the park, after the bottle has been emptied, she tells him she hasn't been nipping from it at all. Every time he passed her the bottle she only pretended to nip from it.

That was the way she was and now he was twice as drunk as he should have been.

IT WAS Pincus who told him about Goldman's. It was the only place in the city that still carried Love Lotion. Pincus and Josh were in the coat closet fumbling with hangers. Pincus was the kind of guy who told dirty jokes at the back of the room during kaddish.

He also told Josh that Kaliotzakis was psycho.

"He's going to get you in the end. I knew guys like that. Those guys are a barrel of laughs until one day they fuck your wife in the tool shed while you're lying in bed with pneumonia. I know what I'm talking about."

Josh nodded agreeably.

"Go to Goldman's," said Pincus. "Tell him Yossel sent you."

Schopenhauer thought that everything was will. You had eyes because you willed yourself to see. You had hands because you willed yourself to grab things. The blood that ran through you was there because of your will *to be*.

At first there was this vague sludge, part Jell-O and part dust, and deep inside, there was some *I* that had willed itself to lick Mimi's toes.

She would only come over if she could get some sleep first.

"Nap from now until 3 a.m. and cycle over," he said.

"Desperado," Mimi said.

He heard her coming up the stairs with her bike. It didn't wake him up because he hadn't ever fallen asleep.

She was wearing pajamas and was all sweaty. The mixed tape she brought over had a song by the Smurfs. At the end of side b she slipped one in by Leonard Cohen. Josh called him Leonard Groan. It was about a girl who blew bubbles, spun her own dresses, and baked fresh bread.

A few months later, someone at a party recognized her. He said there was a plank of wood on the street outside his window. Cars kept going over it and waking him up so when he couldn't take it anymore, he went outside to move it, and a girl on her bike sped past. She was in her pjs, a toothbrush clamped between her teeth like a pipe.

To hear him tell it, that girl just about made his night.

"You promised the chicken was kosher," he cried.

"I thought it was," said Frieda.

"How can you think a chicken is kosher? Either it is or it isn't. Either it's from the kosher section or it's not."

He couldn't understand how she could have done this to him.

Frieda went back to her magazine.

A mother is supposed to be happy that you want kosher chicken.

THERE WAS a man in the mall who sold Mexican jumping beans. He kept them on a mirror under a bright light. They were little beans and they jerked around on the mirror. Chick said that each bean had a little angel inside and the angel had to shit real bad and that was what made the bean move. They were angels born inside little beans. Those beans looked like jerky little shit nuggets.

Goldman was a little old man who wore half a dozen layers of flannel. He was what some would call crusty. Goldman's Emporium used to be a clothing store, but now they sold anything Goldman felt like. He had been in business for almost fifty years and now he didn't seem to care about anything.

"What's it your business what the hell I sell," he would say.

The place was so packed with old stereo equipment and black-and-white TVs that you could hardly move, but in the basement Goldman kept vintage clothes from the fifties covered in sheets of plastic on long tables. There was powder-blue terry cloth cabana wear and striped pants with great big pockets. Under the tables were wooden crates of the Rebbe's Kosher-style Love Lotion.

When Josh laid his eyes on all those dark green bottles, he could have cried.

"What's a little pisher like you going to do with Love Lotion?" asked Goldman.

When he got home, Josh ordered hot dogs and fries, five bottles of Love lined up perfectly on the coffee table in the basement.

When someone starts looking at you like you're greasy, you start acting the part. You move towards them like you're both in a big aquarium of Vaseline. You wear the same pair of underwear day after day until you can pop a boner right through the material. Then it's out there, floating around in goo.

An excerpt from a romantic comedy in progress:

Tony: I wanna lady who'll stick around when I get di-arear. I don't wanna say, "Honey, I got diarear," and have her tell me she's goin out dancin wit her girl friens. I want someone who's gonna mop my fore-head wit a cold wet rag. I want someone who's gonna bring me sandwiches cut into little triangles.

When Josh spread Love Lotion on Mimi's back she made a big fuss about how it was working. She knew he liked that. He would massage it into her skin for an hour, never growing bored. He would pretend that his hands were windshield wipers wiping away to get to some-thing, to make something clear during a long drive.

As he smoothed the Love Lotion into her he thought he heard voices. He thought he heard his mother ask if he had packed a bathing suit because you never know. But it was the Love Lotion. Love Lotion had a way of making a man get very close to his nature.

HE STAYED up late. He was wearing Frieda's pink nightgown at the kitchen table. He was eating raisin toast and reading an *Archie Digest*. His mother came up from the back staircase. She was home from night school. She saw him sitting there.

"Did you find out about the telescope?" he asked.

The club smelled like a cross between a ten-year-old crapping his pants while hanging from the monkey bars and a brand new board game.

Josh ate a whole family-sized box of Raisinettes just to keep his hands busy in a room full of strangers.

"Are you having a good time?" she asked, out of breath.

"I don't like dance music because it reminds me of when my mother smacked me at the pool when I was eight."

"I know that story. It makes me almost cry."

"There's no feeling worse than getting smacked when you're in a wet bathing suit with all your friends around."

She stood beside him and danced.

"Sometimes I hide a latke at the bottom of the cereal bowl," Josh said. He was trying to give Mimi a sense.

"Why?" she asked.

"To surprise myself."

Work was getting so bad he had to go to the bathroom four times an hour to put cold water on his face.

He left there feeling sad and crazy.

At first he tried to buy magazines, ones with glossy pages, cologne samples, and interviews with people who thanked God for everything.

When that didn't work, he did panicky things like making sketches with light blue eyeshadow. He looked out the window and prayed to see something that would set him straight.

There was an Indian girl at the Burger Zoo who was

getting married any day. He couldn't stop thinking about her. He didn't feel young any more. It wasn't that she was so beautiful. There was always the chance she wouldn't get married.

There was a night manager who asked him at the end of every shift to go eat Chinese food with him. The man had the same hair as his father. He kept running into him on the street. He thought the man might be stalking him. It was very sad how he kept asking him to go eat Chinese food.

Chick used to promise to take him for Chinese food almost every weekend.

"You said we were going to go for Chinese."

"Well, we're not going to go."

"But you said we would."

"So your old man's a liar."

It was Saturday night. He fell asleep on the basement floor.

He woke up at midnight and couldn't feel his arm.

FRIEDA SCRUBBING the toilet with his old underwear. What if someone sees?

There were balloons falling and Josh was thinking about taking some home. He thought of how it would make him feel to see them shriveling down to nothing on the basement couch.

He was dancing. He wanted Mimi to see. He thought she had come to the party with him. She was poking those carrots in like that dip was her bitch. She was working that thing like she used to work him. Like the way she used to jerk him while watching TV.

He saw them both walk into the den, which was filled with books from top to bottom. Josh knew that she must have said "Kerouac" to him several times and he was sure he said other names back to her. He couldn't really hear anything with all his dancing.

She was in that room saying things about books and the people who write them. Josh kicked a balloon over to the door. He started dancing just outside the door. He thought he heard, "Kerouac, Kerouac." His feet were wet in his shoes. His face wasn't shaved right. He wanted to pop balloons but everyone would have known what a little boy he was.

If someone had to chop off my arm, I would make sure I got that arm to somehow fall asleep. I would get it good and fallen asleep and I would look them right in the eye while the blood was spraying all over their faces.

EVERYONE RUNS AROUND trying to find a place where they still serve breakfast because eating breakfast, even if it's five o'clock in the afternoon, is a sign that the day has just begun and good things can still happen. Having lunch is like throwing in the towel.

Remember, Josh thought, *it is I who is eating you. It is I who makes you feel pleasure.*

Mimi was lying back thinking about Reggie. She imagined him pumping her on the back of a motorcycle in the middle of a circle of screaming frat boys. She would wake up the next morning on a lawn chair wearing Ray-Ban sunglasses.

"Who's your daddy," demanded Josh.

He thought of telling Kaliotzakis about Love Lotion, but Kaliotzakis was a real meat-and-potatoes lover.

Kaliotzakis would call Love Lotion "gay."

When Josh closed his eyes and smelled the rim of the green bottle, he felt like he could be anywhere. Floating in space, sitting in a closet. Some days, it felt like Love Lotion was all he had in the world.

They were in the washroom at the Burger Zoo. At work everyone washed their hands very carefully and dried them very well. Everyone wanted to kill time.

"I slam the pussy," said the new guy. "I don't fuck around when it comes to the pussy. I step to the motherfucker."

This guy was making Josh nervous.

The new guy grabbed onto the sink with one hand and put the other hand on his left buttock. "You got to make *little* circles." He swirled his hips and smacked the sink. "A gentleman never uses both hands. A gentleman always keeps one hand on the derriere for lower-back support. And you *never* want an arm to get in the way of the camera."

He turned on the faucet and put his hand under the water.

"Feel how wet that is," he said.

When he was finished zoning out in class he thought it was possible he hadn't been zoning out at all but had been showing everybody his penis. And then, afterwards, he wasn't able to remember any of it. The children in his class might have been superb actors and his mother might have begged them all so sweetly that they went along with it, never letting on a thing to him.

His mother had just wanted him to have a normal life.

Mimi coughed out a beautiful white dove and then she died of a heart attack and then the dove died of a heart attack.

Script idea: He's a Latino pop star named Frito. She is

a woman who fears intimacy. When she demands he wear a condom, he waves his boxer shorts about as though fighting off a horrible odor. He says, "Frito don wear r-r-rubber, only the silk."

One day they accidentally walk through a glass window and he yells "Ayyaeah" and then they fall to the sidewalk together.

Josh had been drinking coffee all night. He thought of each cup as the laying down of a stone for a magnificent pyramid that he would one day inhabit.

After his twenty-eighth cup, he set out for her house.

His jingle-bones made him think of his childhood: a father's keys jangling in the door. *I am a golem made entirely of jangly keys*, he thought.

It was three o'clock in the morning when he reached her apartment building, her frightened voice buzzing out of the lobby intercom.

THERE WAS this one time he tried to stare down his father. But that wasn't how it started. They were at opposite ends of the kitchen table, about to eat dinner. It came out of nowhere. Joshua looked at him and his father looked at him back. They kept looking and looking. His father's hands were clamped behind his head. It began to feel too long. His father started to look like something else. Josh started to laugh. The look on his father's face didn't change. Josh rubbed his eyes, still laughing. His mother's meatballs looked weird and too orange.

Josh knew exactly what those people were thinking when they came in for breakfast: *I am eating a good hearty breakfast. This is how my grandfather started his day, with bacon and eggs and home fries and jam.*

But that's where those poor bastards were wrong.

Their grandfathers wouldn't be caught dead in a place like the Burger Zoo.

Goldman's had pictures of the Rebbe all over the walls. The Rebbe was with Dr. J. The Rebbe was with Evel Knievel. The Rebbe was with a very serious and rabbinical-looking Lou Reed. There was even an old sun-faded poster for Love Lotion from the sixties. In it, the Rebbe is holding out a green bottle and Marty Feldman is staring at it with his eyes bulging out of his head. "Make Love, Not War," the caption reads.

"Feldman was the only man who ever made me laugh," said Goldman.

One night he dreamt he was house-sitting for someone. He looked at all the closed dresser drawers and was afraid to open a single one. He got this feeling that he was boring God to death.

Then he heard a voice.

"Don't be a pipsqueak in the Lord's bedroom," the voice said. He was naked and sitting on the edge of

their daughter's bed. When he got up, there were but-
terfly wings of ass sweat on the spread.

Inside the bathroom Chick cracked a bar of soap in half.

Sᴇx ᴀᴛ ᴇɪɢʜᴛᴇᴇɴ had been like eating saltines over the sink in the middle of the night, petting a dog to make someone happy, saying hello over and over, faster and faster, eating a sandwich with tiny bites until you reach a point where you think you're never going to finish.

He pulled a king can out of the fridge at the convenience store. There was a boy inside the fridge. He was stacking the cans at the other end of the shelves. He looked at him as he shut the glass door. He drank his beer later on and thought about the boy. He pretended that the boy made all the beer in a little room back there.

All along there was too much room for something that

could not be there. He got used to it that way but sometimes while he was sleeping, he would wake up and remember something. It made his sinuses clear.

With all their singing about wanting Moschiach, something got stuck in him. Even though he knew nothing was coming, he felt like there should be something coming. When you masturbate, you know what's supposed to happen. Now he was waiting for something that was like coming. He wished they hadn't got him thinking about the sense it made, because now he couldn't get it out of his head and nothing was making sense at all.

JOSH BLEW BUBBLES from his ass. They were brown and looked like they had smoke in them. He prayed to God they wouldn't pop. It was his first date with Gina and he couldn't believe this was happening. He considered trying to pass it off as some kind of shtick.

Someday we will laugh about this, he thought.

"Do you wannashottascotch?" Gina smiled. This was their only inside joke and it wasn't even funny.

Gina worked at a bar. It took her until four in the morning to count the cash because she was always so drunk. When she was finished they walked back to her place and sat on the couch.

When Josh first met her he told her he had just gotten out of prison and was looking forward to dancing with women again. Gina laughed and asked him what they put him in for.

"Aerobicide," he said.

They sat on the couch, her crazy roommate talking to the TV in the other room. Josh didn't know what to say.

"You're so pretty," he said.

"You are too," she said.

She really thought she was being clever.

"I once loved this guy so much I didn't care what made sense," said Gina. "I bit his nose until he cried and even then I couldn't stop."

One night, after all the infomercials had ended, they faced each other in that intimate way people in encounter groups in the seventies must have done when they told of the uncle who took pictures of them sitting naked on a beach ball. They looked at each other while they spoke and they felt cozy and good. They were talking about how sometimes you can reach a wonderful truth based on a lie and, at five in the morning, they held hands.

When Chick was overseas in the army, he gave a beautiful Spanish girl a comb for her hair. Before giving it to her, he placed it under his nose and wiggled his eyebrows like Charlie Chaplin and the girl laughed.

It was the closest Chick had ever come to having a moustache.

The first time she slept with him, as he was dozing off, he thought she put something on his tongue. In the morning, when he ordered his eggs sunny side up he thought he might be on drugs.

HE LIKED jerking off to flappers. These women were all dead but their spirit lived on in his erection and when he came, they died all over again.

God bless the man I saw in the Burger Zoo last night. He was eating out of two brown bags filled with french fries. He weighed at least three hundred pounds. What made me sad was imagining mean teenagers going up to him and saying, "I'm sure your mother's very proud of you," and then high-fiving each other. What would be even worse would be if they left and I was alone on the floor with him. Just me and him. I wouldn't know how much to look at him, the whole place smelling of baby vomit. God bless that man.

Joshua woke up in a shock of stars. He woke up struck with what it would feel like to have his penis pulled off. He couldn't shake the feeling.

Gina got up with him and sat him down on the carpet in the hallway. She gave him a cigarette. At that moment, it looked like the cleanest thing in the world.

"It's cold," said Gina.

Josh smoothed the Love Lotion into her legs.

"Can you feel it?" he asked.

"I think I can—maybe. Is it supposed to smell like this?"

Josh brought his nose down to the back of Gina's thigh. At the very last second, he stopped himself from licking.

There was a hot dog joint around the corner from Gina's house. On his way over, he'd stop in to use the bathroom.

He would force himself to crap and afterwards he would wipe his ass with a determination and vigor that entailed half a roll of toilet paper. He wanted to make sure that he was clean, just in case.

The last time he went over, he had a clean ass for nothing.

HE BURPS and it stinks so bad she feels herself falling out of love. She and the convenience store owner exchange looks. The whole place smells like a New York delicatessen.

"If I'm calling too much I'll stop."

"Don't do this to me."

"I won't call any more," said Frieda. "You'll see. I really won't."

"Everything's a Yiddish opera with you."

"You'll see what is when you have children of your own."

The story he had heard was that there had been the Rebbe, who was a very good man, and then there was his brother Phil, who was always looking for an angle.

The Rebbe tried very hard to make Phil understand what we were on Earth for, but Phil had a taste for the wild side. During the shareholder meetings at Love Lotion, Phil would always be the one to leap up out of his seat and say, "I can go for a malted. Who can go for a malted?"

People would say, "Phil, you have to grow up. Your brother's the Rebbe. Think of him for once." But Phil was just too much of a playboy.

"What have I ever asked of you?" asked Phil.

"Nothing," answered Phil. "They send you a hundred letters a day asking you to cure their hemorrhoids, to make their bad breath go away. I'm your brother and I've never asked you for a goddamned thing and you know it. Just this once, Abraham. This one thing and I'll shut my mouth."

"I love you, Phillip," said the Rebbe.

The first time, it was like struggling with something. He was making Hong Kong action picture faces. The harder he pushed, the more silent things got. He liked to push. He gripped the sides of the toilet seat. Chick and Frieda stood in the doorway, promising him things. Jigsaw puzzles, stuffed animals. It came out of him like a saw, and when it separated it was like having a dog break its leash and run away with your soul in its teeth.

Josh showed up at her house because he just happened to be in the neighborhood. He just so happened to be wandering around in Gina's neck of the woods.

As he was climbing the stairs to her apartment he had this funny idea. He was going to knock really hard on her door and when she asked who it was he was going to say, "It's the Big Ragoo!" He was going to say it like a real New York Italian tough guy who ate cow's balls and salami for breakfast.

He faced her door and put one hand in his windbreaker pocket to get all into it. *It's the Big Ragoo*, he kept saying to himself.

He had never banged on a door that hard in his life. All the dogs in the apartment next door started barking.

A man in shorts and beach thongs opened his door. The smell of Hamburger Helper flooded the hallway.

Josh faced Gina's door and inside he heard the TV. He waited for the squeak of her wooden floorboards to grow louder.

MAN IS TWO. He is holy but he is also a scumbag. He is a sentimentalist but he is also a murderer. He is one but he is also many. Perhaps he is not just two. He is more than two. Perhaps thirty or so.

The yellow kippa was his bad-luck kippa. It was from his cousin Sheldon's bar mitzvah. He was wearing it in the synagogue bathroom when his uncle wouldn't stop tickling him until he hit his head on a urinal.

Hidden in my closet, behind a stack of old board games, is a stuffed animal that I've had since I was a kid. When I was eleven, I used to come on it almost every day. It was a purple rabbit, the fur all stiff.

I kept telling myself that one day I would take it down to the laundromat and wash it. What a day that would have made.

"Abraham, will you look at this?" Phil was dancing around and slapping all the secretaries on the ass.

The Rebbe was tired and old. He was also a little scared of Phil. The Rebbe looked like a kind old fishmonger in a Yiddish opera who was about to have a heart attack.

Phil had them wheel in the prototypes. Phil made a production out of everything.

There were about a dozen dark green bottles. Phil picked one up and brought it over to his brother.

"Ta-da," said Phil.

There on the label was the Rebbe, holding up a bottle and winking right at you. Underneath him, in cursive, was written "The Rebbe's Kosher-style Love Lotion."

The girl walking by said to her friend, "He always, always wears jeans."

Josh tried to imagine what that guy was like.

Someone was playing with the springy doorstop on the other side of the wall. He listened to it. He looked at the grilled hamburger on his plate and listened to that stupid springy sound.

Chick had a fight with Frieda. He stomped into the living room and started taking things off the walls. In one hand was his U.S. Army discharge and in the other was a certificate of appreciation from his students. On it, there was a drawing of Snoopy wearing a graduation cap.

Josh looked at the squares of clean white on the wall.

"Your father's feeling very sad," Frieda said.

He told the pretty girl at the bar that he would like to

take her and her friends out for a bowl of oatmeal sometime. He thought this would create the basis for some witty repartee. He thought she would say, "Oh really," or something. Something coy. But instead she asked him what his name was. He was taken aback. He thought that this was a lucky thing. He said his name was Joshua. She said, "Goodbye, Joshua." He said his name wasn't even Joshua. It hurt the way she said it, "Goodbye, Joshua."

Some nights, I would lie awake and try to recall a smell that was more real to me than the four walls of my room or the open book on my chest.

Tonight it feels like to have once come in her arms is as far away as having once been born.

PHIL GOT DRUNK and talked about all his big plans.

"First I'm going to buy a Winnebago," Phil said. "And I'm going to invite all my friends along. There'll be hot tubs on board! And I'm going to paint 'The Chassidic Playboy' on the side."

Phil wanted to get his own line of lotion going. He was going to call it "Phillip's Secret Ointment." After a few months of tremendous success he was going to put out "Phillip's Secret Ointment: Now with Chives."

If he was a porn reviewer he would use words like "cuntilicious" or "twaterrific." He might have problems with the editor but he would stand his ground.

"The words stay or I leave," he would say.

"What am I going to do with you? The kid's an artist!"

The editor would bite his fist or pinch his cheek, or something like that.

There was a pretty fifteen-year-old girl who babysat him. Once, while she was talking on the phone, she painted his fingernails red. He held his hands out as steady as he could. The girl said he had the hands of a surgeon.

Chick saw Josh's fingers tiptoe across the piano keys. Somewhere in the middle of "The Entertainer," a telephone fell off the kitchen counter.

"Leave my son alone," Frieda said.

Chick wanted to see what the world was like when you were relaxed, so he put on a bathrobe and slippers and took a walk through his neighborhood. He carried a paper cup of orange juice. He wanted to feel like the world was a hospital solarium and the doctors were very pleased with his progress.

Who would tell Chick when to cut his toenails? Who would say "Get out of the tub, already"?

The sun was going down and neither of them made a move for the light switch.

Josh WANTED to show Kay that things had changed. Where there were once black Converse high-tops there were now black combat boots. Where he used to walk like he was trailing yarn between his fingers, he now walked like he was looking for some punk who owed him money.

He waited for her in the booth near the window. When she slid in, there were already five Gitanes squished into the tray like he meant it.

"Sometimes when you keep telling someone you love them," she said, "you have to wonder who's the one you're really trying to convince."

She dropped him off at his parents' house. Chick and Frieda were sleeping. Josh watched *Benny Hill* in the basement and masturbated with his left hand for the first time. He kept at it until footsteps on the stairs killed his erection.

Phil knew how to have a good time. When an old fifties rock 'n' roll tune came on in the grocery store, he would grab his wife's hand and force her to dance with him. It was the kind of thing that old people liked but the cashiers feared. He kicked up his leg and knocked a can of creamed corn right off the shelf.

The cashiers would have loved to destroy a man like Phil.

He dreamt that night his mother was alive. They were fighting in the street.

"I have no more room in the house for toilet paper," he screamed.

"To make me happy," she said.

THE GIRL SELLING KISSES was named Jill. She had frizzy red hair. There was something about her that made him think of a glass of orange juice slimed with ketchup fingers, but she was selling kisses and he was hard up.

Her booth was right beside the haunted house. Jill was busy applying lip gloss as he pulled out a crumpled ball from his pocket and flattened it against his leg into a nice respectable dollar.

"That was magical," she said afterwards.

"Sure," he said.

"No, really," she said.

"No, really," he said.

"We remember moments, not minutes," Josh said to the girl.

He would remember saying that several years later.

He would not be able to picture the girl's face. He would be eating a sandwich.

"I can't concentrate long enough to be in love," Josh said to the doctor. "For the highs I watch Harold Lloyd films. To feel creepy, I listen to ELO."

On the bus ride back he saw up a girl's skirt.

When he got home he masturbated for over an hour and nothing happened.

He shaved his head and walked into the bakery he always went to.

"Hey Kojak," said the Chinese lady who worked there.

Like usual, he ordered one sugar doughnut.

"Did you check the timer?" asked Bob. "Did you even *look* at the fucking timer?"

Bob was holding a big metal strainer of black fries.

All the old people at the Burger Zoo stopped playing cards. Everyone was looking at Josh.

"Do you even understand what you've done?" asked Bob.

The fries smelled like everything wrong in the whole world.

"I'll be your best friend."

He would be holding the orderly's hand from off the side of the bed.

"Joshie, Joshie," an old man would be crying from a bridge chair. He would drive the orderlies crazy with his drama.

Nurses would come in and speak in loud kindergarten-teacher voices. Everything would be hurting so badly. There would be a country song coming from a transistor in the room next door.

They would bring him back from his bath without his moustache and nobody would even notice. It would be like a slip of paper had blown off a desk.

"My mother used to make me take off my pants before trying on shoes," he said, "and now I have many problems."

"You're a fast talker," Jill said, "and from the moment I saw you, I knew you were a good sleeper."

When he woke up in the middle of the night, the blankets in her room looked like an old man's face, thinking.

Jill was in her underwear and she was very shy, but he had talked her into sitting on his chest. He was patting her knees.

"Exactly what's happening right now?" she asked.

Frieda used to remind him of how he thought the strawberries on the cereal box were meatballs.

Outside the window, it was raining. He saw a girl walk by in a dress of paper towels.

THE MORNING that everyone was talking about how the Moschiach had come, Josh was standing outside with wet hair. He was squinting up at the sun. The more the talk kept going, the more real it all got. After a few minutes people were crying right on the street. A horn blew and it made a sound that went all at once: "The president's dead. Your cat's dead. You're really adopted. You're really a girl."

It was happening so fast. He had this funny feeling that it might be him. It might be him that this was all about.

Kaliotzakis took him to a loft party. It was winter and everyone rolled their coats up into balls and stuck them behind armchairs and couches. There was only one bathroom and the line was long. Josh walked out onto the balcony. There was a girl sitting out there all by herself. He handed her his bottle and peed off the balcony. Without the Burger Zoo, his weekends were again his own. He felt free and good.

He brought the girl back inside and asked her to sit with him. Her name was Honey. He remembered her from his street when he was a kid. He looked at her face and felt all the years come back to him.

He wanted her to like him. He didn't know what to say. He pulled out his wallet and poured out everything onto her lap. She looked down at all the cards, money, coupons, and bus transfers. He figured she wouldn't ever be able to get up.

From so far away Josh couldn't tell that Phil was the Moschiach. Phil was standing on a milk crate behind Goldman's.

Phil was a man who got things done. God must have liked that.

"I'm not saying my brother wouldn't have made a fine savior," said Phil. Then he burst out laughing, and so did everybody else. Phil had a way of saying things.

"Christ," said Phil, "can you imagine? My brother battling Satan? Abie was good at endorsements—he had a face you could trust. But to be the Moschiach you need balls! God help us if my brother was ever Moschiach."

"Now you're senile and all but you did some whacked-out shit in the day," the orderly would say. "I seen videos of you yelling at your mother in a shopping mall."

"Get off my bed!"

"I ought to yank the wire on a cruel dude like you."

He used to like talking about his bouts with diarrhea, and he romanticized them way out of proportion. He turned it into a late-night drunken velvet-shirt-and-sunglasses thing. He conditioned himself to go all saucy and fluid just to make sure he'd always have that to talk about.

"With certain people I ramble on because I just don't want to have to hear their voices," said Honey. "With people I like, I get shy and quiet. I ramble on with you because I feel comfortable with you."

Honey was a lonesome little sock of a girl. He wanted to tell her that he missed her terribly all these years, but he hadn't even thought of her. Now that they were together, he felt like he should have been missing her something awful. His regret for having not missed her was overwhelming.

Honey and her sisters would go into their grand-mother's bedroom in the middle of the afternoon and wrap themselves up in the electric blanket. The old woman would chase them out with her fingers full of ointment.

The Moschiach looked a lot like Superman except he didn't fly as much. When he did fly, he'd look down and nod as if to say "Carry on." He was like the Fonz with a twist of Alan Alda's schmuchiness. The Moschi-ach was a shmuchy-face. No one cared about astron-omy. Nobody recorded anything. They had a good-natured fat neighbor named Billy who had died of a heart attack decades earlier, and now here he was, alive and well. He had a lei around his neck. Josh's mother was alive, too. She smelled like her kitchen.

HE REMEMBERED Honey's dirty bare feet all through that summer. He remembered her playing tetherball with her older sister's creepy boyfriends. He remembered her father sitting on a lawn chair in the concrete courtyard, screaming threats at the teenage boys who had the poor judgment to make eye contact with him. There was their sick green car, the back seat covered with empty lemonade cartons, pillows without pillowcases, hair clips, and socks.

Honey's mother came back from her acting classes at eleven o'clock at night, the car that dropped her off blaring Bob Dylan so the whole street could hear. Before she got out, everyone kissed her on the cheek, and then once again for luck.

Honey's mother was the kind of woman who said whatever was on her mind. One time, Josh was walking by when the car pulled up and she called him Jersey Milk from out the window.

"Hey, Jersey Milk," she said.

Inside the car her friends all laughed like it was a part of some bigger joke.

Honey's father was inside the apartment cooking hamburgers. They never had buns.

This is very hard for me to tell. There was one time I was in my mother's room and I took something and I did something with it and now when I'm with girls, I want theirs too and they can't figure it out and I can't figure it out. This is how you become a certain way. This is how you become who you are.

Honey lived in the only full-fledged building on a street full of duplexes and semidetacheds. On Halloween Josh and Kaliotzakis trick-or-treated through the building. Josh had never been in there before. The hallways smelt like detergent and wet dog food.

Honey lived on the top floor near the incinerator. Honey's father answered the door. There was a small pinball machine without legs on the floor of the living room behind him.

Josh was dressed as a boy in the middle of getting a haircut. Kaliotzakis was dressed as Ponch from *CHiPs*.

"Trick or treat," they said.

The apartment had green carpets. The girls weren't there. The father was wearing a lady's bathrobe. He gave Kaliotzakis and Josh one small apple each.

He might as well have handed them a razor blade.

He imagined Honey and her sisters watching TV and living off small apples, their knees pulled up to their chins.

"Now I will show you what happens when you are dead," God said.

"I don't believe you," he said.

Honey went to this horrible daycare where they never let her change out of her wet bathing suit. Her mother sent her there each day with just a thermos full of coffee. He imagined her tap dancing around the play mat for all the boys, never seeing the fat woman in the black polyester pants who wanted to set her straight.

She was dancing the way she did at home on the kitchen table. The fat woman had a handful of slaps for her since the day she first saw her.

Honey's mother planted sunflowers on the front lawn of their building. They looked like faces full of smoke-stained teeth. They looked like dirty yellow ski suits that you find in the schoolyard after all the snow has melted. They looked like a wrapper off a candy that only the sickest kids ate.

We kept going and going until one day the Moschiach showed up and said that things were about to get revealed. We all saw that we were really the size of Chrysler Buildings and sex was about angels dying from the sheer beauty of it all and that the greatest pornography of all was the human imagination.

The Silverman house was burning down and everyone was on the street watching. Their teenage son, Max Silverman, was the only one home when it started. He came out in his bikini underwear and a blanket wrapped around his shoulders that didn't cover his ass. He went running over to his motorbike parked in the driveway and wheeled it across the street, screaming about how his parents were going to kill him.

Max sat on his bike, wrapped in his blanket, watching his house burn. Honey and her sisters sat on the curb in silence. Josh watched them from way in the back, too afraid of sparks to get any closer.

Chick found a little pencil in his coat pocket. He started a sketch on his placemat. It was of the young man in the booth in front of him. After a while, they made eye contact. He waved his arm. The young man sat stock-still and went back to reading his book. For the young man, it was like deciding to not answer the phone.

I drink a bottle of Liquid Paper and say I'm starting over.

WHEN HE WAS TEN, and he concentrated really hard on the sound of the hair dryer, he could hear a hundred voices yelling in unison. His mother called it cabin fever.

He ran through the snow and all he could see was white. It was as if he was dead and nobody could see him. At the convenience store, he walked through the aisles and pretended he was car exhaust.

One night, when they were just getting to know each other, Honey burrowed her head under his arm.

"I'm just going to curl up into your armpit and stay out of trouble."

When the Moschiach arrived, they projected Buster

Keaton films onto the sides of buildings. There was a man giving away hot blintzes. Josh even saw a kernatzle tree. All the subways were made of milk cartons.

Honey ordered half a grapefruit and cottage cheese and he ordered soft-boiled eggs.

"I ought to have my head read," Josh said. "If they don't bring me one of those little egg cups to put them in, do you know what a pain in the ass I'm in for? There's a trick for getting the shell off but I'll be damned if I can remember it."

"Will you relax," she said.

"It's probably not too late to catch the waitress."

Josh told her he wanted to eat her ass. Honey laughed and he said don't laugh because I'm dead serious. He leaned her against the wall and pulled down her pants. He had never eaten an ass before and didn't know where to start.

In the days of the Moschiach, there was a great deal of sex to be had.

Josh once made love to Sharon Stone. They had met in a video arcade. He was playing Missile Command when she appeared behind him and put her arm around his waist. She asked if she could fire.

She had perfect control over her cunt muscles. The room was air-conditioned. There was a soothing hum. She was smiling and chewing gum with her mouth closed. She did this jerky thing where her mouth got all crooked.

She didn't wait for him to come. She started talking about her uncle.

Her uncle had polio when he was a young man and as a result he lost the use of his legs, so he dragged himself around on crutches. Once when he was over he asked her to sit on his lap. His legs were like string inside his pants. The thought of sitting on his make-believe lap scared her to death. She said she was too old for that. He ended up leaving all his money to her cousin. She never understood how he was her uncle in the first place.

Sharon Stone stared at the ceiling, thinking about it.

LOU REED is doing this version of "Satellite of Love." It sounds like a song you make up when you're seven, the way he's singing it. It sounds like the kind of song you make up during a long drive, just to make everybody in the car crazy. It's the kind of song that would have had my father going nuts. My father would have screamed, shut your fucking mouth, why can't you just shut your filthy mouth. *If my father was Lou Reed's father, Lou Reed would have been dead by now.*

Honey's older sister was named Jana. She used to sit in the courtyard listening to the Carpenters on her red tape recorder while smoking cigarettes. She wore a suede cowboy hat with a white feather.

Kaliotzakis and Josh walked by and Kaliotzakis sang:

Smoking makes your teeth yellow
And your breath smellow

You think you're so cool
But you're really a fool

Have you wiped your ass good today?

Out of nowhere, the winter came, and Honey put away her dresses and began to wear stretch pants and carry around tons of pictures cut from magazines in her brown leather school bag. She would schlep it behind her like a tired little kid on her way home from school. That's how she was and Josh would meet her at the subway and take it off her shoulder.

THINKING ABOUT IT and trying to make sure he was feeling something would make his stomach all watery. There wasn't a way you could *know* anything. You couldn't *know* what it felt like to have a penis.

"It feels nice," he imagined saying to the reporter.

One night she showed up after the subways had stopped running. Lying down on the basement couch, she took off her pants, tights, and underwear in one elegant move.

"I want the one-hundred-dollar massage," she said.

When Honey got nervous she would start blinking really hard, like blinking was no longer like breathing, like it was something you always had to be thinking about or your eyeballs would dry up. There were many nights when Josh lay beside her and rubbed the side of her face. He did it with the kind of concentration Frieda used to say wiped away her migraines.

Josh started running into the Moschiach almost everywhere. He figured they had to be robots because no one could be everywhere at once. Maybe the Moschiach thought the same about him.

He had read that the penis was the least oxygenated part of the body. He wasn't sure what that meant but thought it might be why he always felt like it was suffocating.

"You can stay here with me in the basement," said Josh.

"But your dad's here," said Honey.

"You can come through the garage door. It'll be like your own private entrance."

"That's depressing."

"Depressing? No, it isn't. There'll be the sound of thunder and there you'll be."

Kaliotzakis needed a job. He ran through the streets in a cold sweat, résumés flying everywhere.

"Baloney," his mother said when he got home. "Baloney."

He is a grown man and he still reads comics while he eats breakfast.

"I don't want you eating my fruit cups any more," his mother says. "I need them for work."

He finishes the crossword and leaves it out on the kitchen table so she will see.

"Stop leaving your garbage around," she says. "The least you can do is put on pants and warm up the car."

Honey stretched out her hair with both hands to show how far it could go. Her face looked like it was stuck in the middle of a clothesline.

He wished he had just slept over at his grandparents like he did every Saturday night.

In the corner of his parents' bedroom, on the orange shag rug, he cried so hard his whole mouth tasted of carpet.

CHICK HARDLY NOTICED Honey. Sometimes he saw her, and sometimes he didn't.

They wanted the Moschiach to have a cameo on *Baywatch*. He laughed when they asked him.

"How much," he said, still laughing.

"You'll play yourself, of course," they said.

"Oh, I don't know if it would be so appropriate," he said.

"It will be tasteful and it'll be very smart. We'll give you a chance to say a little something, too."

"What would I say?"

"You could just sort of give them the thumbs-up."

"I thought you loved Love Lotion," Josh lied.

"I hate Love Lotion," Honey said. "The basement smells like cough syrup and wet dogs. I want that disgusting crap out of here. Rinse out a bottle and we'll put it on the window ledge as a souvenir."

CHICK LAUGHED whenever a bald man drove by in a convertible.

They sat on the couch in the basement. The left end of the coffee table was broken so it looked like a ramp. Josh put his feet up anyway.

"The thing about coffee tables," he said, "is that they make you feel like you're a part of society."

After several weeks, it was starting to look like a dog with its head cut off. Underneath the overflowing ashtray was a pair of Honey's nylons. There was an Archie comic under a bicycle lock.

"What are you thinking?" she asked.

He was examining the remote control when he noticed a button he had never seen before. It was orange and when he pressed it everything in the room got very dark and quiet.

Honey's sister got her a job at the bank. During the first week Honey spent most of her days hoping the man with the moustache wouldn't show up. Whenever he did, like magic, he ended up her customer. It made her nervous all the time. Sometime after the mid-morning break, a little boy blew into his plastic recorder and she felt a reptile in her stomach flick out its tail.

Just when she was starting to feel all right, hitting the calculator like she was figuring out something deep and important, she saw his old moustached face in line. She saw the line move forward and she pretended that she didn't care. He was a sick old man and that wasn't her problem.

There was a squinty-faced little reptile inside her stomach and it was chewing on tin foil.

Jerry Lewis and Dean Martin made a great number of people laugh, one of whom was Josh's uncle Melvin.

"Anyone who doesn't laugh at those two is a re-tard," said Melvin.

Chick hated Lewis and Martin.

He also hated his brother Melvin.

"If you don't stop farting," said Chick, "I'm throwing you out the goddamn door."

In the morning, Honey ate a coffee yogurt while running around the house looking for an umbrella.

Before leaving for work she stopped to look at him lying there. There was a mason jar of grape juice on the floor beside the couch. Honey placed a yogurt beside it and then she balanced a spoon on top.

THERE WAS ALWAYS so much to do and although everyone loved the Moschiach, no one really gave him much of a hand. He had no time for anything. His wife was starting to get angry. The Moschiach had a wife and she couldn't take it any more.

"You have misunderstood me yet again," the moustachioed man shrieked.

Honey felt something inside twist and unravel.

He picked at something in his thick moustache.

"We will start again," he said. As he said the word *again*, he slammed his strawberry milkshake onto the counter. It sprayed all over important bank papers.

"Please, sir," she said. "You must remain calm."

"I *am* calm," he screeched.

He imagined himself in the old-age home. One day, Kay's daughter, a curious girl just like her mother, would show up.

She would say her name was Jasmine.

She would say that her mother had said many things about him.

Her legs would be skinnier than her mother's.

"It's weird that I'm here," she would say.

There were six of them on New Year's. They sat on bridge chairs in a circle. Honey brought out a bottle of champagne and one of the guys popped it and then no one had anything to say. Honey started to cry as a joke.

The way Honey found blue glass so pretty, even if it was broken, hurt his heart.

"I told you I was making the place more cozy," she said.

Her feet smelled like his childhood.

HE PUT his hand on Sharon Stone's knee and said, "When I was twelve, I jerked off every night thinking about you."

In her head she was trying to count how many cars she had ever driven. She got to eight when the car radio started to play "Shaddap You Face."

"Whatsamatta you," they sang in unison.

They were at the place they liked, the place that served wings.

"Let's ask them if they deliver on Christmas," Honey said. "It'll be so pathetic."

Josh felt like a sick little boy staying home every day. Honey never made a fuss about it because she loved him. At night, he watched TV with the sound turned down while listening to the oldies station.

He always had dinner ready when she came home. It was never anything fancy but he tried to make it look just so on the plate. Tonight he was going to make noodles in a white sauce he would make from white powder. It was healthier than hamburgers and if he had time he was going to go out and buy some broccoli. He asked Chick if he wanted any, but Chick only liked the orange sauce.

The next-door neighbor's two-year-old was playing with the doorstop on the other side of the wall. He made dinner and listened to it.

It was like someone was asking him something, over and over.

He started making little figures out of clay. He planned to make enough men one day for a chess board. He lined up all three on the coffee table. When Honey got home and saw them she touched the side of his face. She was like a tough guy with a big, big heart. He brought out the plates of food like he was spinning them on his index fingers.

Honey's head was tilted and she was mouthing the words to a song. He was wearing a cowboy hat and fighting back the nagging whine of mid-afternoon winter diarrhea. She needed a black coffee and he needed a clean bathroom. He wished he was alone. He wished to God he could just walk into the closet and sit down amid all her shoes and think.

She was saving the Miami Beach ashtrays. The phone was ringing. He couldn't find any paper towels.

"I was happy to be left alone," he said.

"I was saving those," she cried. "I've been saving those since I was a little girl."

Josh felt like a psycho when he stared at her face too long, in the kitchen, on the bus, while she was sleeping, naked on the fold-out couch over the winter blankets. Honey was so lost and gorgeous, he could just die.

She had this smell and Josh thought what an incredible thing to have a smell and how wonderful it was that he was there to smell it. They got drunk and moved in and out of the things they said and they truly meant them.

THEY HAD NEVER actually been formally introduced. He knew it was stupid to think, but it was like the Moschiach had been purposely avoiding him. The most he ever got was a quick nod.

Josh ran up to him on the street and smacked him on the back. That was what everybody did. Everybody smacked everybody on the back in the early days of the Moschiach.

He dug it out of his pocket to show the Moschiach. It was a switchblade but instead of a knife, his penis popped out.

"Cute," the Moschiach said.

Josh refused to wear a white shirt with the suit.

"Light blue is very in these days," he said.

At the wedding, Honey kept telling him that they

should dance. She was worried her family would think she wasn't normal.

"This sherbet tastes like aftershave," Josh said to the little boy seated beside him.

Everyone did this one dance move. They did it in unison like the Solid Gold dancers. Josh danced like he was trying to catch a glass of tomato juice that was falling off the fridge.

Honey talked to her aunt who sat in a chair the whole night.

"If I could do it again," her aunt said, "I wouldn't be such a hotshot."

After they finished dinner, she picked up his napkin using the tips of her fingers.

"Look at yours," Honey said. "Now look at mine."

"Normal," she said. "Not normal."

"Well, I had a perfectly lovely time," he said as they drove home.

"She has braces, for God's sake," she said. "When I was a little girl, I wanted braces so bad I made some out of pipe cleaners."

Her hands were balled up into the tiniest fists. He could have fit the two of them in his mouth.

JOSHUA AND Honey decided to get their own place. In every apartment they looked at, Joshua imagined himself sitting on the toilet. He imagined Honey singing in the kitchen. It had to feel just right. It was going to be like their own little tree house with pots and pans and plumbing.

He thought about it a lot.

Josh wanted to give the Moschiach a big hug, just to cut through all the weirdness.

He saw him standing outside the diner. He was getting his shoes shined while reading the paper.

"Phillip," said Josh.

"Amigo," said the Moschiach.

"I used to feel so many awful things when I got into bed at night," said Josh. "But now that's all changed."

"Good stuff."

"I just wanted to let you know that I'm really glad for everything that you've done for everyone."

Josh reached in to give him a hug, his chest crushing the newspaper.

Men in dark sunglasses jumped out of the diner and pulled Josh back.

"Some business," said the Moschiach. He made this cute what-can-you-do face. "They treat me like I'm covered in magic dust."

Josh smiled and the Moschiach smiled back.

Josh was going to take his old bed to their new place. Honey and he could use it as a day bed. He saw himself lying in it in the afternoon, hands behind his neck, thinking brave and beautiful thoughts. He took down some of his old shelves and posters, too.

"Don't dismantle me the room," Frieda would have said.

"It's just stuff you'll never use," he would have told her.

He woke up that morning and put on cowboy boots and jeans. It was the middle of the winter and he would be lugging a bed up two flights of stairs but he saw himself moving in with Honey wearing cowboy boots.

His boots made this noise on the roof of the van that made him feel like Paul Newman.

He imagined Frieda sitting on the edge of her bed, playing with his Rubik's Cube key chain.

Honey only had sixty dollars to her name. When she got into the moving van, she gave him thirty. It was in a wad. A real wad. Money was such bullshit, but money divided that gracefully moved him more than a kiss.

Chick was smacking the side of the TV. He looked at the scrambled picture with disgust.

"I guess I'm gonna probably get going," said Josh.

Chick kept looking at the screen.

"Honey and me are pretty much set up there," said Josh.

"I never understood her name," said Chick. "Do you think about honey every time you say 'Honey'?"

"I guess I did in the beginning," said Josh.

"I still do," said Chick.

Just when it seemed like all was lost, Harpo honked everyone in the room with sleeping gas from out of his horn and Chico said, "Good work, now let's get out of here," but Harpo sprayed Groucho, too. Then sprayed Chico. Then he lay down in a beautiful woman's arms and sprayed himself. Everyone was asleep when the credits rolled.

"One thing I'm going to want is a desk," he said. "I want a big sonofabitch where I can spread out index cards and Harlem Globetrotter stubs."

He wanted a desk on which he could throw down a five-hundred-sheet package of paper like a big slab of raw meat. He wanted a desk that could support a typewriter and all the mess like a stoic South American colonel who's got grandkids playing on his back.

Honey was waiting in the van. Josh ran back inside. Chick was leaning against the kitchen counter with his arms folded.

"I'll have to put you in a smoke detector," said Chick.

Josh offered him a lift to the video store and Chick said sure.

Josh was eating a plate of eggs and bacon at the diner counter. He was wearing a pair of boxer shorts and an undershirt. Frieda was dressed like a waitress. She was making coffee and singing kooky songs.

Kaliotzakis came in and sat beside him.

"The Moschiach says," said Kaliotzakis, "that you're ruining it for everyone. This whole thing that's taking place—it's not for you."

"What are you telling me? Wow, this is some egg they make!"

"All I'm saying is that you shouldn't *be*. It's for the good of the world."

Josh knew it was bound to catch up with him. He gave it a shot. He squinted his eyes and tried ceasing to be.

"It's no use. I can't do it."

"That's because you don't want to do it. You have to want to do it. You have to want to not be."

"Well, let's say that I can't?"

"That's why you have to make yourself."

"How can I make myself when the me that's making me agrees with the me who doesn't want to not be?"

"You have to find a *me* that can get the whole thing going. Listen, this business isn't for you! Angels? Eternity? Bah. You'll be climbing the walls in a couple of years. A guy like you needs something to put his hands to. A wart to pick. A trade to ply. Try again, and think about what a rip-off this whole thing is and how you'd be better off not to be."

Josh's hands were in tight little fists that meant business. He squinted his eyes even harder. He gritted his teeth and held his breath.

"Hey, don't shit your pants!"

Josh's mouth let out a "pffhht" sound. He smacked the counter. He smacked Kaliotzakis's back.

"It's good to be here," he said.

Acknowledgments

I am indebted to Golda Fried, Hal Niedzviecki, Heather O'Neill, Ken Sparling, and Alana Wilcox for their early encouragement, editorial guidance, and inspiring work.

Thanks to the following publications in which excerpts from this book have appeared: *Exile, Matrix, Blood & Aphorisms, Fish Piss, Front and Center, Broken Pencil,* and *a carwash the size of a peach.*

I would also like to thank my family and friends for their love and support.